Infinity

Jo-Anne Joseph

Print ISBN 978-0-620-76699-9

Edited by: Shana Vanterpool
Proofreading by: Jenny Dillion from Indies Ink
Formatting by: Abby Formatting and Web Design
Cover design by: Dani Rene

To my son,
Everything is possible.
Constant as the stars above,
Always know that you are loved,
And my love shining in you,
Will help you make your dreams come true,
Will help your dreams come true.

From Constant as the Stars above
by Rob Hudnut and Amie Roth

Of Love

What shall I say of you oh love?
Are you the sweet kiss of the morning dew?
Or the first rays of the healing sun, awakening me from the deep.
Are you the sweet smell of roses in the Spring time?
The sparrow's first song with whom my heart does sing.
The feeling of the grass under my feet on my mountain top
The smell of home after a long adventure?
Or the feeling of safety after being lost for eternity?
And yet I cannot afford you all these honours, oh love.
For within my canvas of breath-taking colour,
There is a darkness that threatens to engulf me,
Until all my colour is swallowed up in your abyss,
And the fires of hell call to me.
How can something so beautiful be so sinister at the same time?
And then I realise, oh love,
You are both a blessing and a curse,
The light and the darkness,
A force of nature,
neither asked for, nor which one can live without,
to ensure survival, until your task is complete, and then, like a betrayal you leave,
And the longing for you once more remains,
Only never to be filled again,
Empty,
Hollow,
still longing...

- Brian Joseph

2017
Present Day

"Even the moon needs the sun to shine,
How then will I survive, without you?"

-Jo-Anne Joseph

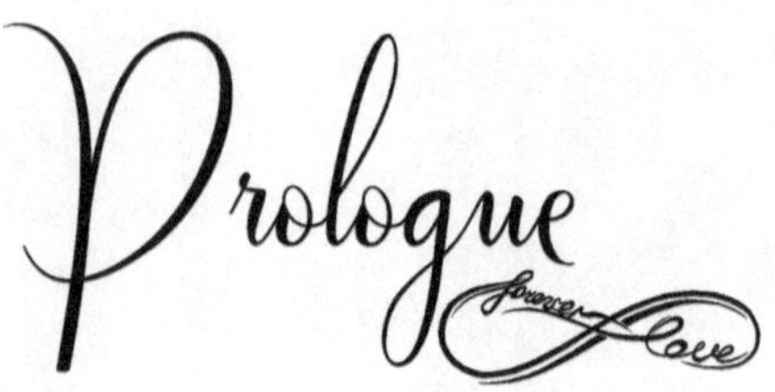

LEAH

I cannot remember the exact moment I fell in love with him, but I knew I was irrevocably in love, deeply and completely, in every sense of the word. I felt it in the very fiber of my being. It wrapped itself around me like tendrils of silk, entrapping me in its web. I fell hard and I fell fast, there was no denying it. But I tried to deny it, for a number of years, especially to myself, but even so I always knew it deep down in my soul.

I called it a passing phase, unreal, self-created, a young romance doomed to an inevitable end. But in quiet contemplation, when it was just the moon and me on quiet evenings, when the wine ran dry and the tide was high, I gently admitted that I missed everything about him, from his gentle morning kisses, his subtle smiles and the brief touches we shared. Those were always the highlights of my younger days. I loved curling up to his side, my head on his chest listening to the quiet of the morning and his heartbeat. It was pure joy and contentment. When he would call me unexpectedly in the middle of the day, just to tell me that he missed me, I would smile at hearing his voice but pretend it didn't affect me as much as it did, but it always did.

I was only a teenager back then but yes, I knew I loved him and I knew he loved me too. The man, who said he didn't know how to love, loved me and I knew that a love like that would last forever. I didn't want him to leave me and he didn't want to leave either. I cared for him. I cared so much and I would have followed him to the end of the earth in another lifetime. Those were younger days when the weight that life placed on one's shoulders was not that hard to bear.

"I love you, you know," he would whisper, and I would look up into his soulful brown eyes that reminded me of milk chocolate believing him because I knew beyond a doubt that he did.

"I want to run away with you, away from here, away from everything that says we shouldn't be together," he said.

"I wish that life was that simple," I would smile wistfully at him.

Then he would kiss me as if his life depended on the union of our lips, and I kissed him in the same way, never wanting the moment to end.

Somehow, we both knew it must.

Those were younger more carefree days. Days I sometimes wish to have back. I sneer at my insanity and put my cup of coffee back down on the brown hardwood coffee table. I get up and lock the door of the hotel room, making sure to check it twice. I make my way to the bedroom, my feet sinking into the plush white carpets.

I look at myself in the vintage mirror above the whitewashed dressing table and despite my imagination I am still the same woman I have always been. The same brown eyes that see the world in various shades stare back at me and the same brown, long, curly hair falls wildly around my shoulders.

I stopped trying to tame it a long time ago, he liked it best this way anyway. I seem to have shrunk in the time I have been here. Maybe the sadness is consuming me from the inside, like a silent cruel monster. Maybe it would devour the whole of me one day. I walk across the room and lie on the luxurious king size bed, sinking into the comforter, alone. I close my eyes and he's right by my side, as if he never left.

He stands before me in the rain, shirtless, anxious, swearing to stay there no matter how long it took, unless I leave with him.

"I can't. I can't do that." I am frustrated and afraid that someone will see or hear this scene unfolding between us.

"Why can't you?" he pleads. "If you love me, come with me." Anger burns within me. We are in this situation because of him.

He falls to his knees in front of me, his tears getting washed away in the rain.

"I do love you, I always will, but I can't leave with you, not after everything that's happened." It hurts to recall. It hurts to

feel.

He looks at me, the pain evident in his eyes. He seems to battle with himself for a moment about what his next move should be, but he gets up and strolls down the pathway slowly. He pauses and turns to me. My heart hurts to see him hurting.

"I would die for you, Leah, give it all up for you. I thought you wanted the same things I did."

I did want the same things but not after what I had seen. How could I trust anything he says to me? He was not the kind of man you gave it all up for. Still, I wanted to run to him, touch his slouched shoulders and tell him that I'd forgiven him. I wanted to feel his lips against mine just one last time, to feel his arms wrap me in his warmth. I wanted to do all of that and more but I didn't. Instead, I walked inside my house, shut the door behind me, and sank to the floor in a heap of regret.

The next morning, he didn't call me like he usually did, and over the next few weeks, I could no longer call him mine. We went our separate ways, and I swore that I would never give another my heart the same way. I bid goodbye to the only man I had ever loved.

I wake up and the sunlight streams into the large hotel room windows. I'd forgotten to draw the curtains the night before. I hadn't even gotten under the blankets. I sigh, remembering my last thoughts, my only thoughts lately. Who am I anymore and why did any of this have to happen to me?

My family and friends continue to reach out to me

every day and despite my reluctance to speak, they pursue. There are some things in life for which there are no words and so I stopped speaking. I did not need to say anything they all didn't already know. I am broken, most likely beyond repair.

The nausea I've been feeling over the last week washes over me again and I need some air. I get out of bed and open the large glass door leading onto the small balcony. The cool morning breeze greets me and brings with it the smell of the Atlantic Ocean, which stretches before me endlessly. Its sparking blue beauty is mesmerizing. The golden sand stretches for miles. I breathe it in, deeply and desperately, welcoming its calming sensation into my lungs. When the calmness fades, as it always does, I plop down into one of the two plush loungers on the spacious balcony and I let the morning air warm me up and the sea air engulf me. My muscles ache from exhaustion. The pain and discomfort is a welcome sensation. I do not need comfort now.

I need to forget, even if it's just for a little while. Reaching under the small glass coffee table beside me, I pull out my third bottle of Jack Daniels Whiskey this week, noticing with irritation, that it is only half-full. I reach for a glass but find it shattered on the floor. What the heck, I muse and bring the bottle to my lips.

I must forget.

That is the thing about memories, it weaves its web into your consciousness and refuses to let go.

I close my eyes and let the warmth of the golden liquid burn my tongue and my throat and maybe, just maybe, it would numb my senses too. It is sharp and smooth all at once.

Whiskey, the great storyteller, the maker of fools, my new best friend.

After a quarter of the bottle is down, I feel a whole lot better. My muscles start to relax and my head feels a bit fuzzy. The heat of the mid-morning sun gives me a headache and so I take another swig. How long have I been lying here? Do I care? I lie back in a drunken daze praying for oblivion, but instead I unwillingly set the memories free, I let them wreak havoc with my mind. I give them life and power. They physically hurt but they have to come. There is no way to end them and if I am honest, I don't want to.

"Guess who?" He comes up behind me and catches me by surprise, picking me up and whirling me round until I'm chortling. I'm dizzy by the time he sets me down.

"You're crazy, you know that, right?" I giggle. He pulls me closer, his eyes meeting mine.

"I am crazy, crazy about you. I missed you," he smiled.

"I missed you too," I murmur, nuzzling into his neck taking in the scent of him, earth and sun. I hop up and wrap my legs

around his waist, my hands around his neck. We fit perfectly, we belong together.

He backs me up against the nearest wall and kisses me hard, I kiss him back, and let the intense sensation and his lips consume me. He leaves one hand around my waist and slides the other under my white t-shirt. My eyes fly open and heat fills me as I pull him closer to me, wanting more. He kisses me gently, and then sets me on my feet, his eyes still ablaze.

"I'll have you, Leah, someday," he grins as he backs away from me, leaving me reeling. "Just not today." He winks and saunters off.

That night, we made out in an almost empty cinema. I'd never felt that way about anyone, not ever. I'd dated, but I've never felt like I could give my heart and soul away without a thought for the repercussions. On our way home, the rain came down hard and when we pulled into my driveway, he slipped off his jacket throwing it over my head.

"Here, cover up Princess, I'll meet you inside." He opened his door and ran over to my side to do the same. Ever the gentleman.

I ran into the house, made my way to the kitchen, and turned on the kettle. I was soaking wet and so glad that no one else was home that evening. He joined me a few minutes later, slipping his hands around my waist and drawing me to him causing a shiver to course through me which had nothing to do with our wet clothing.

"I love you, you know?" he whispered in my ear, making the hairs on the back of my neck stand on end. "Always," he hissed as he kissed my earlobe.

I could barely breathe. Everything in me needed this man. "You have no idea how much I love you too," I whispered back to him.

Love is a strangely wonderful thing, magnificent even, but if you're not careful, it can crush your soul, someone once told me, and I understand that now.

After spending the last week holed up in this hotel room, drinking myself to oblivion day and night, I can finally appreciate the sentiment.

Love does crush the soul, fortunately, mine doesn't exist anymore.

2001

"Between words left unspoken,
And deeds left undone,
So much of everything is lost."
-Jo-Anne Joseph

LEAH

In less than a month, my final year of high school will be over. I'll be starting college, and I can't wait. I'll miss my parents, of course, but unlike most of the young women I know in this town, I want some independence and some sense of freedom away from the comforts of home. When I was younger, I was always the quiet sort with my nose stuck in a book, staring at the world with fascination, waiting for a story to unfold. "She is far too mature for her age." I often hear people saying. "She's a dreamer," others offer. I appreciate the analogy, although a dreamer was far from what I am. I realized early on that I could not be comfortable with only having dreams. I want more for my life. I want to be more. I want to experience life, wholly and completely, and that is just what I intend to do.

Books have always expanded the way I view life. They take me to places I have never been to. They cause a deep yearning in me for new and more. One day soon, I want to visit the places I read about. I want to experience a rainy day in London, to walk along the cobblestone paths that lead to fresh and fascinating places. I want to stand in front of the Great Pyramids of Giza, and experience a sweltering day in the desert of Egypt. I want to go on a pilgrimage along the Camino de Santiago in Spain, and get blisters on my feet, and ride in a Gondola in Venice. I knew that it would all begin with starting college hundreds of miles away from home. It would be a venture into the unknown. I want to find myself, to be myself. To find what is missing in my life, because frankly, at almost eighteen, I do not have a clue as to what exactly is missing.

I, Leah Jones, want an identity of my own. I crave it.

I don't want to be the valedictorian Leah.

I don't want to be the smart and beautiful daughter of Mira and Garrick Jones.

I want to be me.

I want to get away from this entire small town and its narrow-mindedness. It isn't any one specific thing. It is a restlessness and thirst for more.

My parents are amazing. They are close to perfect, the sitcom kind who still dance to no music and insist that we sit together for breakfast and dinner every night. They spent time with my brother and me when we were growing up, and really take the time to get to know us, as individuals, and not just as their children. My father works in the construction field, and builds the most magnificent structures and renovates houses to perfection. My mother is the local librarian, but she is far from the nerdy, bookish sort. There isn't a day that goes by where she isn't wearing a colorful scarf on her head and a Bohemian dress. I got my love of reading from her and my sense of adventure from my father.

"Mom, are you home?" I shout, as I fling my duffle bag onto the floor in the foyer. She will get me for that later.

I can hear the television on in the kitchen. I never understood the logic of having a TV in the kitchen, but my mother did.

"I don't want to miss a show, Leah," she would say.

"I'm in here, kiddo!" Mom shouts over the noise of the television.

I have no doubt that she is watching a daytime soap opera. She is addicted to those shows lately. I walk into the kitchen and salivate at the smell of grilled cheese toast.

"Ah, Mom, you know me too well." I smile and sit down at the kitchen table with my arms outstretched. A laugh falls from her mouth and she comes over to kiss me on the cheek. She smells of home.

"How was your day, honey?" she asks.

I give her an enthusiastic thumb up, only to have her roll her eyes at me in response. I guess I'm rubbing off on her.

"It was good, Mom. I hardly had any weed today," I joke.

"Ha, ha," she fakes a laugh, playfully pinching my cheek.

"We need to talk, honey." She looks over at me, raising her eyebrows while piling a sandwich on my plate and handing it to me.

"That is never a good idea, Mom," I tease, already distracted between chewing. Mom makes the best grilled cheese toast, the kind where the melted cheese drips out from the sides. But comfort food always means that something is up.

"Leah, behave," she scolds. "You remember Kevin's friend, Leo?" She doesn't wait for me to respond before continuing. "Well he's moving back to town and doing up the old farm house. He'll be moving in with us for a few weeks while he's working on his place."

I stop chewing and meet her gaze.

"What? That is crazy. We don't even know the guy all that well. We haven't seen him in years, and doesn't he have any family of his own?" I don't bother to hide my exasperation with the idea of it.

"Things aren't great between his mother and stepfather and him. It's been like that for years now, Leah, and well… we are the closest thing to family he has at the moment."

"Mom, there are hotels and motels, B&B's—" I start, but get a glare from my mother, which causes me to drop the subject.

"He won't be a bother, Leah. He just needs a place to stay for a while. I offered in fact, despite his protests, and I will not have you making him uncomfortable. Leo is a good young man."

"What about friends? Can't he stay with any of them?" I question, causing her to eye me incredulously. I give up, knowing that winning this battle is not in my favor.

"Leah, I have never been in favor of Leo's behavior in the past, but deep down he's a good young man and he's really pulled himself together. He's got a job at the local law firm and he needs our help temporarily, it really is the least we can do for an old friend."

I relent, knowing there isn't much I can do about it. Finishing off my sandwich, I get up from the table to leave.

"Mom, he's not a good young man." I roll my eyes dramatically. "But if it's what you and Dad have decided, then I guess that's it."

Leo Williams never seemed to fit in here in Greyton.

His family moved here when he was ten-years-old. He looked and played the part of the boy from the wrong side of the tracks well. His father died when he was just a toddler. His mother remarried, and I suppose the relationship between the two of them was always strained. I knew all of this because of my brother Kevin.

Kevin always said that Leo grew up too fast and had the added responsibility of taking care of his younger brother. He and my brother became good friends. He was six years older than me, and I can't deny that I'd always been fascinated by him from the first moment I laid eyes on him.

I'd been walking to school one day when I saw Leo stop outside old widow Mrs. Francis's house. Most people steered clear of her, especially the children in the neighborhood. No kid in his or her right mind would ever go over there, especially not alone. Nevertheless, there was Leo Williams, making his way nervously over there with what looked like a sandwich bag. I found that strange. Leo didn't seem like the type of boy who did things like that. I wanted to follow him and ask him about it, but I didn't think that would go down well. So instead, I wrote, Leo is so mysterious, in my diary later that day. I remember falling to the floor sighing adoringly, conjuring up all the mysterious things he did and hoping I would build up the courage to ask him about that someday.

Leo was handsome back then. The boy with eyes that reminded me of milk chocolate, so brown you could imagine tasting them and black hair that fell over his eyes. He had a crooked smile which only rarely surfaced. The part of his face that fascinated me the most were his dimples. I tried to talk to him a few times, but he stared at me without saying anything. I always left feeling deflated, my young heart broken. I couldn't understand why he never liked me. I was a nice enough girl.

All through our childhood, he was there. He practically lived at our house. I suppose it was an escape for him. He would sit and watch soccer games with my dad and Kev. He didn't speak much, especially to me, and he wouldn't say more than an occasional Hi, or Bye. Still, he was nice to look at and so I looked, until Kevin told me to get lost for being weird.

I didn't care much about the fact that we weren't friends as I grew older. He was trouble anyway, according to everybody in town. A few years ago, a year before Kev went off to college, Leo took off to live with a relative and it was as if a weight lifted off my chest. I did not know why he got to me, but he did.

I close my eyes and take calming breaths. I will be on my way to college soon, and Leo Williams will be the last of my concerns. I sigh and find myself yawning. It has been an exhausting afternoon.

"Lee-bear," Dad's whisper rouses me from my sleep. I didn't even realize I'd dozed off.

"Hi, Dad." I yawn, getting up from the bed and rubbing my eyes. "What time is it?" I ask groggily as I look out of the window, taking in the dusky sky, painted in deep shades of orange and red.

"Around six-thirty, and almost dinner time it seems." He laughs, motioning to my rumbling stomach. I laugh at myself, patting my stomach.

"So, Mom told me about your talk earlier," he looks at me knowingly.

"Yeah, I guess I was kind of rude to her, I should apologize."

"It's just a temporary arrangement, Leah. Just until Leo's place is sorted. Every act of kindness, no matter how small, is for a greater purpose, Leah, because someone needs it or can't do without it, even if we can't understand it initially." He bends down to ruffle my hair playfully.

"I know, Dad, I'll try harder."

"Now, that sounds more like my girl," he smiles, leaning in to kiss my forehead. He turns to leave, his hands in his pockets. "He's moving in this weekend by the way," he adds with a grin.

I flop down on the bed, groaning.

"That's tomorrow, Dad," I sigh. He chuckles and leaves the room.

I hear him descend the stairs, and then the faint sound of Mom and him talking in the kitchen filters up to me. They are no doubt celebrating their victory. My parents really were the nicest people on the earth to let *that* person into our home. I get up and make my way to my bathroom, which thankfully, I will not have to share.

"Nice, Leah, be nice," I remind myself.

I brush my teeth, comb through the knots in my long brown hair, twist it up in a messy bun, and then make my way downstairs for dinner.

I get up early the next morning, and throw on a pair of denim shorts and a t-shirt with the word HOSTAGE sprawled across my chest. When I make my way downstairs, Mom rolls her eyes and swats me on the ass with a dishtowel.

"Very mature, Leah," She motions to my t-shirt.

"Smells amazing," I shout over Air Supply playing on her iPod, ignoring her comment. The smell of grilled bacon, fresh toast, and sausages tantalizes my taste buds.

"Where's Dad?" I question, finding it strange that he

isn't already gulfing down the food Mom made.

"He drove over to Leo's place to have a look at it. You know how Dad gets about these things."

Because of my Dad's profession, I can imagine his fascination with this new project. He's already thinking of ways to bring the place to life, as he told us last night at dinner.

"Already?" I sass. "I thought I would at least have a few hours of peace and normalcy before—" I cut off when I hear movement behind me, and I see Mom's face flush all the shades of red that exist. I just know I've stuck my foot in it. I mouth a *sorry* to her only to be met with a glare.

She rushes over to immerse Leo in a hug. My father stands awkwardly behind my unwanted guest, looking like he wishes the ground would open up and swallow him.

"It's so good to have you here Leo," Mom fusses. "Please sit down." She offers Leo the chair beside me. He takes a seat and his presence is intimidating and seems to fill the room.

"Hi," I turn to Leo, plastering on my best fake smile, and dropping it instantly when his eyes land on mine. I can't help but gawk at the specimen before me. His black hair is tousled, his face, which I am certain must be chiseled by the gods themselves, is covered in a short beard. His black t-shirt and jeans fit him like a second skin. He is gorgeous. There is no disputing that.

"Hey." He nods, frowning at me and turning back to my Mom.

We sit at the table in silence as my mother places plates before us. While we dig into breakfast, I can't resist stealing glances at the man beside me, inhaling deeply every time he moves. He smells good, I admit, despite myself. It's something fresh and earthy.

My parents chatter to him about what he's been up to over the years and all the amazing things he has planned for the property. I finish my breakfast quietly, zoning out of the conversation which fails to hold my interest.

I'm seeing Owen today, sexy bad boy Owen Devlin, who I happen to be dating. I practically drool at the thought of him. Those soft brown eyes that turn a girl's knees weak, those even softer lips which have claimed mine countless times, that ass...

"Leah," Mom hisses, and judging by her infuriated tone, I assume she's been talking to me.

"Yes, sorry Mom." I mumble, not appreciating being torn from my fantastic daydream.

"I am just saying that we are *all* so pleased to have Leo staying with us. Aren't we?" She lifts an eyebrow, warning me.

"Over the moon," I sigh, not able to hide the sarcasm.

"Well, thank you, Mr. and Mrs. Jones, and you, Leah," he adds. "This means a lot to me," Leo says, his tousled hair falling slightly in front of his face, and his lips slowly turning up into a smirk, revealing the deepest dimples I have ever seen. I notice the tiniest butterflies in my stomach and quickly stand up to leave. He may look like a Greek god but he is still Leo Williams.

"I've got to go," I announce, placing my plate in the washbasin. "Bea and I are going to the mall. She'll be here to pick me up soon, so you don't have to drop me off, Dad."

"Don't be too late, Lee-bear, we can see a movie later," Dad winks.

"Sure, Dad, I love you." I bend to kiss his cheek hurriedly and hug Mom, who is now fumbling at the basin.

"Bye, Leo," I hiss, throwing my curls over my shoulder.

"Bye," he retorts, not bothering to look at me. He has a nerve.

I don't know why this guy gets to me the way he does. We never really talked in the past, and we're hardly acquaintances, even though he practically lived in my house for years. But he did get to me. There has always been something about him that rubbed me the wrong way. Maybe it's because of all the times he ignored me as a kid, looking at me like I was the most insignificant thing to him. Whatever it is, I do not like Leo Williams very much back then and I didn't see that changing anytime soon. I leave the house hurriedly and stand on the porch, grateful to be away from him.

Bea pulls up outside my house a few minutes later in her black Audi hatchback. She got her wheels when she turned eighteen, which is typical of my best friend who doesn't wait for anything. I hop in, and our drive to the local Mall is spent recapping the morning's events and me venting about my now awkward home life situation. One light at the end of the tunnel though, is that I would be meeting Owen later. I practically drool again at the thought.

"It's not going to be that bad, Leah," Bea exclaims, her jet-black curls bouncing as she wiggles in the seat across from me, her brown eyes wide with excitement. Boy does my best friend love dramatic situations. We'd just placed our main orders with the waitress and I am sipping my lime milkshake, sighing melodramatically.

"He's like this charity case for my Mom and Dad," I snap, earning us a few disapproving stares from the people at the table next to us. "I don't know why they couldn't just adopt a fucking pet."

"Whoa, Leah, that's a bit harsh, don't you think? It's just for a few weeks. Isn't it?" she asks. "And you've

already told me he's a lawyer or something. That is far from being a charity case, Leah." She rolls her eyes at me.

"I know that, Bea, but I don't care. I don't want him in my house period. It's a fucking inconvenience," I growl, ignoring the head shakes of condemnation we're receiving from the tables around us.

Our main orders arrive, a garden salad for Bea who is constantly watching her already perfect figure, and a chicken Caesar wrap for me. The food is delicious and distracts me for a few milliseconds.

"We haven't seen this guy in years, Bea, and then he shows up out of the blue and he's moving in with us."

"Temporarily," she reminds me.

"I know. I guess I am being a bit harsh. Truthfully, I didn't want that kind of annoyance in my last few weeks at home." I sigh when she gives me the eye.

"So, is he hot?" Bea giggles.

"What, Bea—" I flush and I have no idea why.

"He's hot, isn't he?" she asks, laughing.

"A little, not much, can we just drop this?" I beg, feeling a flush creep up my neck.

She throws her hands up in front of her face in mock surrender, but her smirk tells me she'll be bringing up this conversation again.

"So, you're meeting Owen later?" she asks with an edge to her voice.

I roll my eyes. "What is it?" I ask, frowning.

"I've told you before, he's not the kind of guy I want to see my best friend spending that much alone time with." Her response is one I'm already used to. I know she doesn't like Owen, but I do. She just doesn't know him the way I do.

"He has a bad reputation with the ladies Leah, and he has this vibe I don't like." She stares into space for a while. "I don't know, like he's there, but isn't." She sighs.

"It's just a high school thing, Bea. He's hot and I want someone to pass the time with until I leave," I promise.

My response is met with a nod but I know she doesn't agree. Owen is a complicated guy. I can admit that. He's undeniably hot, but he definitely has a reputation for being a playboy. I didn't want to go out with him initially, but a few months ago, I decided to give it a shot. It isn't anything serious. We were just two teenagers fooling around. My phone beeps and I stare at the screen, and let out a sigh.

Owen: Babe, something's come up so I'm not going to make it today.

Me: It's cool.

But it isn't cool. This is the fourth time he'd cancelled in two weeks. I frown, pushing my plate away from me. Bea pins me with that knowing stare I resent sometimes.

"He cancelled." I fling my phone back in my handbag.

She nods knowingly. "Well, that means we get to go shopping, doesn't it?" she asks.

I smile at her and try not to let this disappointment ruin our time together. We finish our meals, and spend the rest of the afternoon shopping for graduation dresses. I suppose there is nothing better than spending time with your best girl. And I'd scored big time in that area.

LEO

I've always been a loner and a *troublemaker*, according to everyone. My dad died when I was five-years-old. My younger brother, Liam, was only a few months old when he died. I don't remember enough about my dad, only that he had an infectious smile and a laugh which I sometimes dreamt about in my early childhood. Although the memories of him have slowly faded over the years, I do know that it is possible to miss someone you love irrespective of the length of time you had with them.

Losing my dad didn't just affect me. He left a gaping hole in my mother's heart and in her life. That gaping hole consistently grew over the years and became the abyss she was trapped in. She lived, but barely existed. She turned to alcohol to drown her sorrows soon after he died and I cannot recall a time when she was ever sober enough to be a mother to us. The woman that used to bake and play games with me was long gone, and in her place was a cold, crude replica. She never laughed, unless she was mocking me, and she didn't care whether there was enough food in the house or whether we had the necessities children should have had. I had to make do with what there was because complaining wasn't an option.

By the time I was seven-years-old, I was fending for myself and taking care of my little brother too. I made sure we stayed out of her way. I did not want to hear how I was as useless as my father was, abandoning her when she needed him the most. I wondered if she ever thought about the things she uttered so thoughtlessly. I got the sense that she loathed me, but I didn't care, not really. I guess that after enough time of people treating you like trash, you start to believe you are and don't bother hearing it.

My mother remarried just after my eighth birthday. A man named Theodore, or Ted, as we all knew him. He was the first of many assholes to come. Ted was the first man my mother dated after my father died. At least the first one I knew of. He worked at a hardware store and drank even more than she did. He was always in a bad mood and I was usually the reason for it. I did not know that simply existing could anger someone until I met Ted.

He would come home and I would be at the kitchen

table doing my homework, when suddenly I would get a slap against the back of my head for not doing the dishes, or some other task I had not done.

The beatings were bearable, I gladly took it so Liam didn't have to, but the emotional torture wasn't. Being made to feel like I didn't exist or matter was agonizing. That is what kept me curled up, with tears soaking my pillow every night. I wished to be anywhere but there, anyone but me. I didn't have such luck.

Eventually, Ted left. He apparently couldn't handle my mother and her little bastards any longer. My mother dated anyone she could for about a year after that breakup, until John arrived, he wasn't like Ted. John appeared to be a good man. He worked at the local school as a teacher, and made an honest living. He tried to teach us good morals and insisted that we all attend church and sit together as a family for dinner as his god intended. But I've learnt that appearances can be deceiving. My mother kicked him out the day he decided to bring home another man to share in their bedroom activities.

After that, she was always wasted. She upgraded from booze to some heavier stuff. She went out with one man after another and each time she thought he could be the one. She was aging fast. Her silky black hair hung limply on her shoulders and her black eyes no longer held the light it used to. I didn't recognize her anymore. She was pathetic.

"You know I love you boys, right, Leo?" she'd ask me, taking a drag of her joint and blowing the smoke in my face, slurring her words until I could barely comprehend them.

"This time, we're going to get someone better, I promise," she claimed.

She never understood that I never wanted anyone else to be better. I wanted her to be the mother she should have been. I didn't want to lift her head from a pool of vomit every single night. I didn't want to hear her sexcapades until the early hours of the morning. I didn't want to wear second hand clothing and broken shoes to school. I didn't want to be my brother's caregiver, instead of his friend. I just wanted a normal life, no drama, and she couldn't give that to me. She refused to even try.

When I was ten-years-old, she met Lawn, and after just a few months, he'd convinced her to sell her house, our house, the only thing my father left us, and move to a small town called Greyton. She did it, all in the name of love. Love would beat her senseless almost every night but love was bringing in the bacon so I was reprimanded if I dared speak against it. I was just a child anyway. *"You don't know anything about the struggles of adulthood,"* she'd tell me.

"*Don't you try and spoil this for me, Leo*," my mother

threatened, her lips bleeding and the skin below her eye cut after another one of Lawn's displays of love.

"*It's just his temper, is all,*" she'd try to convince herself, giggling hysterically.

The woman had lost her mind a long time ago. I was good at evading beatings from Lawn. I kept my head low and did as I was told. The only time I felt a semblance of normalcy was with my best friend Kevin.

It was my first day at school, and as usual, my shoes were busted and my jacket worn. The teacher asked me to stand up and greet the class and tell them a little bit about myself. I dreaded this. I didn't like talking to people, and I didn't like the way they stared at me with pity, suspicion, or disgust.

"I'm Leo Williams," I stammered, looking nervously up at the students in front of me.

"And I'm a street rat," someone finished.

Laughter overtook the room and the teacher battled for control.

"That is enough, Aiden," she shouted at the young boy who'd said that.

"Where'd you get that jacket from, Williams? The dumpster?" He laughed, and everyone joined in.

I hated this new school, I hated this new class, I hated the teacher for doing this to me, and I hated Aiden, whoever he was, but mostly I hated that it always had to be me. I was always the butt of jokes, the outcast. I clench my fists while fighting back the acid building in my throat. My face blushed and I shook some hair into my eyes to hide the tears, which were quickly forming.

"Cut it out, Aiden," said a tall boy with glasses. He glared at Aiden, and I saw the other boy shrink away. "I wouldn't want to have my mother talk to your mother about it, now would I?" the boy with glasses continued.

The teacher told me it was okay to go back to my seat. The boy with glasses ushered me over.

"Hi, I'm Kevin Jones, nice to meet you." He smiled kindly and extended his hand for a shake. "You can sit next to me." He motioned to Aiden's seat.

"Oh no, I couldn't," I stood wringing my hands together anxiously.

"It's empty, why the hell not?" he asked, and when I turned back to the seat, Aiden had vacated it and was now sitting in what should have been my seat at the back of the class.

"Thanks." I smiled. "I'm..."

"Leo Williams," he finished.

His brown eyes were friendly and I was grateful for him sticking up for me. I wasn't used to that. For the first time since my father died, I finally felt important. Important enough for this kid, who obviously held a lot of sway at this school, to not only remember my name, but stick up for me.

"It's great to meet you, Kevin Jones." I smiled.

I had a feeling we would be friends for a long time.

After that incident on my first day at school, we were inseparable. We played together all the time, and he invited me over to his house. His parents were everything parents should be, and I enjoyed being in their company. Lawn didn't mind me visiting them. It was good for his reputation to be associated with the Jones.' I loathed the association and how he would come to pick me up every evening and act like he belonged there. The Jones' didn't seem to mind either. They were friendly people and were glad to have me around.

Kevin had a younger sister, Leah. She was an annoying girl with a shrilly voice and eyes that were much too big for her tiny face. She would look at me, practically drooling, and she made me feel like a science experiment, or worse, a double cheeseburger. The girl would eat me alive. I was sure of it. She had it in her. I told Kevin that once, and he laughed at me.

"She's just a kid, Leo. She fancies you, you know? Why don't you just make her day and greet her the next time?"

So I did. I greeted her and watched her cheeks heat up. She ran away on those gangly legs, and I could hear her in her room noisily hyperventilating. Children were so dumb sometimes.

I didn't think I was dumb, but as it turns out, I was.

"We're in ninth grade, dude, come on, we got to go to this party. Can you imagine the girls there?" I laughed at my friend and he rolled his eyes.

Kevin had that whole good-looking nerd thing going on. He

hated these parties but would often go to keep me in check. I was your typical bad boy from the block making out with most of the girls who were willing to. Kevin and I being friends didn't make sense to everyone else, but we were always together. He was so much more than a best friend. He was my brother. He was the guy that came over to my house with a take-out without me asking. He sat on my dirty floor without giving a shit about how dusty his pants got.

"Come on, Kev?" I did my best puppy dog impression and he relented.

"Fine, just some booze, we kiss a few girls, and we split, right?"

"Right," I agreed.

Jordan's house was just two blocks away, but Kevin's dad insisted that he drop us off. Arriving there was like entering a P Diddy video, well minus the naked chicks and stuff. The booze was low key but we'd been here often enough to know where to go to find some.

"Kevin, Leo, my guys." Jordan slapped us on the backs. "Glad you two could make it."

He passed us two beers and it tasted like heaven. Underage drinking was so worth it. I laughed to myself.

"Make yourself at home guys," He said, and we grab some seats near the pool. That's when I saw her. Lucy Smith. Man was she hot. She was in tenth grade and at fifteen, she'd filled out in all the right places. I shoved Kevin and he groaned.

"You're not serious, that chick is dangerous with a capital D."

"People assume that about me too." I laughed, walking toward her, her pretty eyes searched mine. She smiled at me and beckoned for me to follow her.

That was the night I lost a lot more than my senses, in the back seat of Jordan's mother's car.

And here I am back in Greyton, only this time I am going to do things differently. I will make something of myself and prove to myself that I am so much more than people think I am.

LEAH

High School is finally over. It's a lot to take in, the fact that I won't be doing the same monotonous things I have done for the last twelve years. Being at home suddenly sent my emotions into overdrive. I notice everything about everyone, like how my Mom chats for an hour straight to my Dad every single day after she got home from the Library. She still giggles like a teenager and I squirm at the thought of what they were discussing.

My Dad left at the same time every day and he sang *Eye of the Tiger* off key in the shower. Things I hadn't even realized before because I used to leave the house before everyone.

And then there's Leo, the new addition to the family. He rises at the break of dawn every day. He runs for an hour and then gets back to do pull ups on a tree branch in the backyard. His hair sweaty, his muscles straining. He seems to lose focus of everything when he is working out. After his torturous workout, he sits on the grass and meditates for exactly fifteen minutes, his eyes closed and in deep awareness. It doesn't matter if it is too chilly outside or if it rains, his routine never changes. He showers for twenty minutes and he moves around so stealthily that I never hear him making his way downstairs for breakfast. He doesn't wear anything with color. He is always in black or gray and most of all, he hardly ever smiles.

The one time he did smile was because I spilled milk on my father while staring at him, wondering how he kept his hair so wild. He looks at me straight in the eye, smiles and winks.

Leo Williams winked at me and I could barely breathe.

"You are so beautiful, Leah." His hand slides up my shirt and cup my breast. His kisses intensify, and the want is evident in his eyes and rapid breathing. I try to focus, but I can't. I'm not feeling it and I can't lead him on. We're in the backseat of Owen's car and I can think of a million places I would rather be.

"Owen, I can't, not now," I blurt out.

He instantly stops kissing me and looks down at me in confusion.

"You're never *not* in the mood," he accuses, slightly

out of breath.

"I know. I think it's just the fact that my whole life is changing, Owen," I lie.

He straightens up and looks at me almost angrily.

"Do you still want to be with me, Leah?" he questions, straightening himself.

"I do Owen. I just can't do *this* right now," I hiss, upset that he would jump to such conclusions. And what the fuck is with the aggressive tone? "Just take me home," I order, buttoning my shirt.

The drive home is quiet. I lean over and kiss him on the cheek when he pulls up outside my house. My display of affection is met with a sneer I want to slap off his face. He's cancelled on me countless times. Why would he be surprised that it's come to this? "I'll see you over the weekend, I hope," I tell him as enthusiastically as I can muster.

"Yeah, sure," he responds without even looking at me.

I jump out and watch him pull off. I sit on the front porch staring out at nothing. What is wrong with me? Owen is a great guy, isn't he? And he likes me. I just haven't really liked him a lot lately and I wonder if it has something to do with one tall, dark and handsome houseguest.

I decide to call Bea. She'll know just what to say to make me feel better about this situation. She picks up on the first ring.

"Can you come over, Bea?" I sigh. "I really need my friend."

"I'll be there in about ten minutes, babe."

I take a seat on the porch and lean against the pillar. I suddenly have the worst possible headache. Bea pulls up exactly ten minutes later.

"What's up?" she says, hurrying up the pathway to sit beside me and pulling me into a hug.

"It's everything, Bea, things were great and now I just can't stand Owen. I feel like I barely know who I am anymore," I say.

"It's just the stress of all the changes to come, Leah. It's normal to be nervous and also to reconsider certain things in your life," she says. I know she's talking about Owen, and as much as I want to be annoyed at her, I can't help but feel that there is some truth in her words. "Don't be so hard on yourself, "she continues.

"It's not only that, it's also this whole business of Leo moving in with us. Everything is just complicated with him around. I feel like I can't breathe, like he's in my space suffocating the life from me."

"It's temporary, Leah, he will be gone before you know it," Bea offers

"I really want Leo Williams out of our lives now, Bea," I trail off when I notice her eyes fix on something behind me.

"Hi, ladies," a voice grunts and I freeze. Not again.

"Oh shit," I silently mouth to Bea, who looks like she's seen a ghost.

"Leo, I didn't..." I start but I know I have stuck my foot in it yet again.

"It's okay, Leah, I wasn't trying to eavesdrop on your conversation." And with that, he walks past us toward his car.

"Go after him," Bea whisper shouts at me.

"I don't want to, Bea," I say stubbornly.

"Leah, just go!" she growls and I get up and catch up with him just as he's about to put his car into reverse.

"Leo, I'm really sorry, that was such a rude thing to say," I offer sheepishly. I wring my hands together in front of me, rocking on my heels.

"Look, Leah, it's fine," he grunts.

"Where are you headed?" I ask, feeling dumb even questioning him about something like that.

"My place," he sighs running his hands through his hair. I have come to recognize this as his way of easing his frustrations.

"Can I join you?" I ask, surprising myself, but wanting him to say yes more than anything.

"Don't you have plans for the day?" he asks coolly cocking an eyebrow at me and motioning to Bea leaning against her car.

"No, I'd like to come," I say eagerly, feeling like such

a horrible person for saying something so thoughtless.

He nods and leans over to open up the passenger door, his eyes never once leaving mine, and in that moment, I can't breathe, I can't look away.

"Get in," he says simply and runs his hand through his hair, giving me a peek at that dimple that lights up his face when he smirks.

I wave at Bea and get in, and he reaches across me to close the door brushing against my breasts in the process. There it is again, the butterflies as I catch that familiar scent of *him*. He takes off toward his house which isn't too far away. The knuckles on his hands are white as he grasps the steering wheel and there are beads of sweat gathering below his hairline.

"I'm really sorry, Leo, I just, well, I don't know you very well. You've basically avoided me like the plague my whole childhood, and well, and it's just going to take some getting used to, having you around all the time," I say softly. I don't mean to be so apologetic but even I can admit when I've been a total bitch.

He looks at me and I swear I stop breathing for a second. His eyes are gentle, not hard like they were before.

"I know, Leah. I know it's awkward having someone else living in your house, but I need you to know that I appreciate what your parents are doing for me and it is temporary." I notice that his grip on the steering wheel visibly lessens.

"Still, I shouldn't have said it like that, it wasn't necessary," I mumble looking outside the window as the other cars whizz pass us. I need to look anywhere else but at him.

"Let's just start again," he offers. I face him and he smiles, his dimples surfacing again and causing my heart to skip a beat. Those dents are so difficult to ignore.

"Hi, I'm Leo Williams, and you are?" He extends a hand to me. I take it.

"Leah Jones." I smile at him.

"Nice to meet you, Leah Jones." He grins.

"Likewise, kind sir," I tease putting on my best Southern belle accent.

He starts laughing at my efforts and I swear in that moment that his laugh is one of my favorite sounds.

There is something magical about his place. It reminds me of something out of an old 60's movie. It's like I've gone to sleep and woke up somewhere else. Yes, it is pretty old and run down, even with the work my father and Leo have already done on it, but, even so, I can see the potential. It is beautiful and I can see why someone would want to own it. It is truly a treasure.

An old oak tree sits in the corner of the front yard, and I imagine that the family that lived here before probably had a swing set up. I envisage a couple sitting on the wrap around porch on wicker chairs, smiling at their children running around. It is a beautiful thought. The grounds, though overgrown with grass and weeds now, make it all feel incredibly otherworldly. The house itself is large but not overpowering. There are two floors and the whole structure is made entirely of wood, with large windows which overlook the town. The whole place is completely foreign in this town. I have only ever seen these kinds of houses in movies about places overseas. It is incredible. Greyton is a small town and most of the houses are small farm style or colonial cottages. There is nothing as lovely as this.

"It's beautiful," I marvel, walking toward the stairs to the porch.

"Thank you." He smiles. "Watch your step, though. Those things aren't steady enough yet." He motions to the stairs.

I sit on the second step and look out at the yard.

"You're going to love it here." I smile.

He grins and looks around. "I sure will."

I can see his love for this property shining in his eyes. I can see his adoration and his pride, and I think that it is amazing that he is sharing this with me.

For the next hour, I read on my Kindle while he pulls

at weeds and clears out the walkway.

He tells me that the last construction work will start next week and will not take more than a week or two to complete. I feel a sense of disappointment that he will be gone so soon. I don't understand how an opinion you once held about someone can change in such a short period of time. But, my opinion of him definitely has changed.

As we make our way home, later that day, I feel sad that the day is over. It is inspiring to see someone so passionate about something, like Leo is about making something of his property. I wonder if I will ever be that passionate about anything.

It became a daily ritual for me to join Leo when he is at the house. We would talk about everything or nothing at all. Sometimes I'd just sit under the old oak tree and read a book. Sometimes he'd ask me what the book is about, and at other times he would seem distant, like he is there but he wasn't. I never pry in those times. But I can't deny that I like the way his jeans hug his ass, or how the skin on his bare chest almost glistens after a hard few hours of labor in the sun. I didn't want to notice these things, but I did.

"Hey, lazy bones," he shouts, startling me. "How about you give me a hand and pass me that hammer?"

he asks, grinning at me.

I walk over to pick up the hammer. He is holding up what looks like a small banister, his muscles strain to hold it up. My heart rate seems to increase and my palms get excessively sweaty whenever I am around him. I reach up and pass the hammer to him, our hands touching for just a brief second. It is nothing sensual. Just me passing him a hammer, but boy did it feel intense.

I wonder what it would feel like for him to run his fingers over my arms.

What am I thinking? This is insane. I turn around quickly and go back to my spot under the tree, pushing all thoughts of Leo and his touch out of my mind.

"You okay there?" he asks an hour later.

"I'm great," I retort as calmly as I can muster.

He offers his hand for me to take it. I let him pick me up. I suddenly slip and lose my footing, and the next thing I know, he grabs me until I'm leaning flush against his hard chest. I can't help but look up into his beautiful eyes, with the longest eyelashes I've ever seen. He stares at me intently. His full lips are slightly parted.

I want to feel his lips against mine. The tension is thick between us. We are so close. Our lips are nearly touching. Does he feel it, too? My heart beats rapidly in my chest. I can hear it in my ears and it's making me dizzy. He clears his throat and thankfully breaks the moment.

I take a step back slightly out of breath and light-headed.

I cannot think like this, not about Leo.

"Hey, Leah." Leo smiles as he walks up our front pathway. I've been trying and failing to concentrate on the book before me. It's supposed to be riveting but instead I find myself reading the same line a few times and it had nothing to do with the story. My mind has been all over the place over the last few days.

"Hey, Leo." I glance at him briefly and nervously tuck a stray curl behind my ear. He's wearing a gray t-shirt and matching sweatpants. Why must he look so damn good all the time?

He sits down next to me. He's so close that our thighs brush against each other. I'd like to think that we've become friends over the last few weeks, so I can't understand why having him sitting next to me feels odd and strangely unnerving. I can't forget that moment at the house, but he hasn't brought it up since then. I am starting to think that I may have imagined the intensity of the moment and the undercurrent of electricity which flowed between us. The air was heavy with a tension I thought we were both feeling.

"You okay?" he questions, looking down at me with

those eyes that seem to penetrate my soul.

"I am," I say tersely. I look at my book again, not wanting to meet his gaze. I feel him shuffle next to me.

"Sorry, I didn't mean to pry. You just seem a bit down," he says hesitantly.

"I said I am fine, Leo. Please excuse me, I have some stuff to do," I spit the words at him, getting up abruptly and making my way into the house and slamming the door behind me. In that moment, I don't care if that is a rude thing to do or an immature way to behave. I stand against the door to calm my racing heart.

I don't want to talk to Leo Williams. I run upstairs and go straight to my bedroom slamming the door behind me, grateful that my parents aren't home yet to witness my meltdown. I sink to the floor against my door and the tears fall. I don't know why I'm crying. A knock on my door startles me. I know it's him but I don't think I can manage another conversation with him right now.

"Go away." I sob quietly. I rest my head against the door, wrapping my arms around me protectively.

"I—I just want to talk, Leah," he pleads, uncertainty lacing his voice.

"Well I don't feel like talking to you Leo, so leave me alone!" I shout.

It is silent for the longest time. I hold my breath, afraid that if I don't, I'll say something I will regret. I hear his retreating footsteps and let it all out, flinging myself onto my bed, allowing the soft comfort of my space to soothe. This is not right, Leo is my brother's best friend, and it sure as hell is not fair to Owen. I have to think about what I am going to do about this, about my irrefutable feelings for Leo. The way I feel about him is overwhelming. I barely know him well enough to feel this way, but I do. I close my eyes and take deep breaths until I'm calm enough to drift off to sleep.

I get up and darkness shrouds my room. The curtains are still open. I get up quickly, brush my teeth, tie my hair up in a messy bun and make my way downstairs. It's unnaturally quiet. I see Leo in the living room, reading something.

"Are my parent's home yet?" I ask.

"Your dad called, he completely forgot about a networking dinner tonight so he and your mom will be late. I ordered pizza." He motions to the dining room table.

"No, thanks, I'm not hungry," I respond and turn to ascend the stairs.

I hear his footsteps behind me and I take a deep breath.

"Leah, wait, have I done something?" he asks. I stop

and turn around. He's standing a few stairs below me. His eyes hold a desperation I have never seen before.

"No, you haven't, why would you think that?"

"Well, you seem pissed off with me for some reason," he continues, climbing up another stair. He's standing so close to me now, we're almost at eye level. I can't exhale, it's like the space is suddenly closing in around me.

"I need to go." I turn away from him quickly.

He reaches out and gently catches my hand. The power in that simple touch shocks me. I pull my hand away from him. He looks as shocked as I feel. I cannot do this. I cannot stand here pretending that nothing is brewing between us. I run up the stairs, my heart pounding in my chest as I enter my bedroom.

The fact that I am falling for Leo Williams is undeniable now. This is crazy, I know it. He is a family friend, my brother's best friend, he is strictly off limits. The soft knock on my door startles me.

"Leo, just go away!" I shout.

"Leah, just talk to me," he appeals.

I walk to the door and open it. He's leaning against the doorframe, his arms over his head, his hair falling over his eyes. A small frown creases his handsome features. I want to place my fingers over that line, to sooth it away.

"I don't want to talk about it, Leo..." I start backing

away from him. I stop when he starts walking toward me, his dark clothing only accentuating his demeanor.

He wraps his arms around me suddenly. I want to fight against his hold on me, but I can't. This feels too good. He feels too good. I wrap my arms around his torso and lean into him. He smells of sandalwood, earthy and fresh. He nuzzles my hair and I hold him tighter. I don't want to break away. He tilts my face up to his. He looks as pained as I feel, and I want to stop breathing, the moment his lips meet mine. His kiss is gentle at first, as if he wants to etch the feel of my lips into his memory. I feel it in the fiber of my being, it fills my senses and I moan into his mouth. It is all it takes for his kiss to intensify. His hands are in my hair holding me in place. I meet his kisses fiercely, fisting his t-shirt. He breaks away from me suddenly, backing away looking like a deer caught in headlights.

"I'm sorry, I'm so sorry, I shouldn't have done that," he says, backing away, and I am left reeling from the intensity of the kiss and the absolute insanity of what just happened.

He leaves my room without another look back and I stand there without words to explain what just happened between us.

I lie awake in bed for a long time after he left my room. I hear him enter the bathroom and I imagine how his tousled hair looks wet and how those taut muscles flex as he clears the steam off the mirrors. I wonder if he is thinking about me this second. I can't help myself. I can't believe I didn't notice my feelings toward him changing. But I am more confused than ever because I don't know what exactly he feels toward me.

He isn't at breakfast the next morning and I wonder if he still wants to go to my graduation dinner tonight. My mother invited him last week. I didn't think our kiss would change anything between us, but I wasn't so sure now.

My Mom is in a cheerful mood and my Dad left earlier than usual for a site inspection.

"Where's Leo?" I ask Mom nonchalantly.

"He had to go to work early today. Why?" confusion evident on her face.

"Oh, I just want to check if he is bringing a date tonight, we have to inform the organizers about any changes in number," I lie.

"I doubt that. He hasn't been seeing anyone as far as I know, although I know a lot of young women who would like to change that in this town." She laughs.

I inwardly cringe. I have to make sure I wear something exceptionally sexy tonight.

"I'm off to see Bea, Mom." I finish my whole-wheat toast and wash it down with some hot chocolate.

"See you later, honey."

Bea and I spend the rest of the morning shopping and doing our nails and hair at the salon.

"You seem distant today," Bea observes over lunch.

"I have a lot on my mind, I guess," I say forking my food around the plate.

"You mean you have a lot of Leo on your mind?" she teases.

"What? Why in the world would you even say that?" I ask defensively.

"Oh, cut the crap, I have been to your house when he's around and I see the way you look at that guy." She laughs. "I've been your best friend since kindergarten, Leah Jones. I know these things."

"He's probably taken, Bea, and anyway, he's just bad news," I say flippantly.

"Says who?" Bea counters between bites.

"Everyone, Bea,"

"And since when do you care about what people think?" she coaxes. "You have to make your own deductions about people, Leah, not listen to petty gossip and bullshit," she says.

And I know she's right. If I've learned anything, it's that assumption is the mother of all mess ups.

"I suppose you're right, Bea, but that still doesn't

prove anything, I mean come on, I can't handle a serious relationship, which is something a person Leo's age would be looking for. Besides, isn't he the type of all-round bad guy you are constantly warning me against?

She rolls her eyes.

"I'm barely eighteen, Bea. I'm only just graduating from high school. Next year I am off to college so it wouldn't make any sense to pursue a relationship anyway," I say, more to convince myself than her.

"Well, you'd better figure it out, and soon, you've got crazy Owen on a string and you're definitely hot for Leo," she says matter-of-factly.

"I am not hot for him and Owen isn't crazy," I gasp.

"If you say so," Bea smiles. "So, is Leo a good kisser?"

"BEA!" I laugh. There is no way I could keep this or anything from her. She has a Leah sixth sense. I cover my face hoping my blush won't show.

"It was that good, huh?" She giggles and I playfully swat her.

"It was incredible, nothing like I have ever felt before. It will be difficult to get him off my mind." I smile. The truth of my words cause an ache in my chest, one I know comes from the fear of falling too deeply. I like Owen, there is no doubt about that but what I feel for Leo cannot be compared. He is a man that can break my heart and yet I willingly offer it to him.

Mom and I spend the afternoon fussing about and creating havoc upstairs. I have not seen Leo all day and my anxiety levels are hitting the roof. The phone rings downstairs and I rush down, but Dad beats me to it.

"Hi, Leo," he speaks into the receiver. "That's a pity, it's no problem at all, we'll catch you later, bye." He places the receiver back in place and is startled to see me when he turns around. "Hey, Lee-bear, I didn't see you there," he laughs.

"Was that Bea?" I ask, already knowing the answer.

"It was Leo. He called to say he couldn't make dinner tonight. Liam's down with a cold and he has to be there," he explains.

"Oh," I say, not bothering to hide my disappointment.

I quickly climb the stairs and rush into my bedroom, slamming the door behind me. It's not like I even care if he's there or not, but that does not explain the lone tear that falls onto my cheek as I do a final makeup check. He didn't even have the decency to tell me himself.

LEO

I'm watching Liam shooting hoops, sitting on the sidewalk. Liam is a good kid and I'm so glad that he has a better life now. I hadn't seen Liam for a few years after my mother's husband Lawn kicked me out. I had nowhere to go except to my mother's sister, Dale, in another city, hundreds of miles away from my brother. I didn't want to leave but I had no choice. I had nowhere to go. When I left town, social workers finally removed my brother from my mother's custody and he's been staying with my father's sister Dawn since then. They take care of him and love him like he is their own. They never did have children and Liam has filled that place in their lives.

Thinking back to my own childhood, I can peg every negative experience in my life to the night we lost our dad, which is why I swore to always be around for Liam. Things didn't turn out that way at first. Dawn and her husband Trevor were your typical suburban upper-class and forbade me to see Liam after they were granted custody. They believed I was a bad influence and that I'd mess him up the way my mother messed me up. No one bothered to see beyond all that.

My time away, despite the fact that I couldn't see Liam, let me get on my feet, which is why I am here now, back here in Greyton. When I graduated from high school, I was lucky to immediately land a job in the administration department at the law firm where Dale worked as a paralegal. My aunt was generous enough to pay for my law studies. I didn't even think law was for me. It always felt like a stuck-up kind of profession, but I realized that I could help people through family law, especially kids like Liam and me.

My mother laughed it off when I called to tell her about it. She called me a loser and proceeded to remind me that I didn't have the brains for something as smart as that. I never called her after that. Dale made me realize that I could do just about anything I set my mind to. She was my saving grace in so many other ways. She instilled values in me which were lacking and made me believe in myself again. She and my mother were polar opposites. It is strange how two people can grow up in the same household and turn out so completely different. Their parents died just before my mother married my father. She never married and didn't have any children so she took me as her own. I missed her so much these days. *I will call her later.* I want to be better and do better and maybe even give my brother the opportunities I'd never had. I just wish I could shake off the voices inside that constantly make me second guess myself. I am proud of what I'd achieved so far, but I couldn't help but think that I would end up just like my deadbeat mother someday.

I wasn't just in town to fix up the old farm house. I'd gotten a job offer to practice at a local law firm, having passed my bar exams. I want to get the experience and then move to the city the first chance I get. I intend to turn the farmhouse into a guesthouse or boutique hotel. It is beautifully located and would meet the needs of this growing tourist spot. I don't see myself surviving long-term in Greyton. The narrow-mindedness would suffocate me.

I have always been different from my mother. Unfortunately, the people in this town never seemed to accept that. Even landing the job at the law firm was a huge effort. The stuck-up partners couldn't see me as anything but a bad boy. Yes, I fooled around when I was a kid, got into some trouble with the wrong company but it was my rebel stage. I was fortunate that one of the senior partners liked me and decided to give me a shot. I guess it didn't matter what papers you had behind your name, if you came from the wrong side of the tracks, your reputation generally precedes you.

I guess no matter what I do, I will always be seen as Lara Williams' son to everyone in this town. In the grander scheme of things, I would never be respected because of my origins. There were only two kinds of people in the world: those like the Jones's and those like the Williams. I never saw a difference between Kevin and me, but when it comes to Leah, I don't think her family would be so keen on her seeing someone like me, despite how I'd turn my life around.

I missed Kevin. Although I doubt he'd be my shoulder to cry on if he found out that I'd kissed his little sister. I think I broke a bro law there. So that's the reason why I'm here instead of there, with her. She doesn't need that kind of confusion. That piece of shit, prep boy Owen is more in her league anyway.

"Hey, Leo, come shoot some hoops with me!" Liam shouts.

I get off my ass and run over to play with my brother. It's late afternoon and I should be getting back to the Jones' but I want to stay here. I just called Mr. Jones to tell him I couldn't make Leah's graduation dinner. It is a family thing and I am clearly not family. I am far from that. It's a cowardly move, not telling her myself but I don't know if I would be able to deny her if she'd asked me to come.

Leah Jones. I actually kissed her last night. I don't know what got into me but it was a long time coming.

She's beautiful, smart, funny, and all the things a woman should be. Her wild brown curls surround her like a halo and her deep brown eyes are full of soul. When she smiles, I swear the whole world should be bowing at her feet. Her curves are probably the envy of many. She's perfection but she's not made for someone like me. I haven't been able to keep my eyes off her the last few months. I feel something for her I can't really explain. I've been with a lot of women in my time but this attraction to Leah is different somehow. I have succeeded in not getting emotionally attached so far. I don't do feelings and I don't do love. I don't think I've felt much of anything, except with Dale, Liam, and Kevin.

Still, I was up all night thinking about that kiss, how her body fit against mine, how she smells like summer rain, her beautiful eyes and soft lips melting into me.

"Bro, you're killing me here." Liam breaks through my thoughts.

"Sorry, L-man," I say getting up to join him.

We play until the late evening and I am surprised that Dawn isn't out here busting my balls about keeping Liam out so long. I take him inside and give him a hug goodbye. Dawn quickly comes forward to greet me and she's pleasant. She looks a bit too made up for an evening indoors, and I assume they're having friends over.

"Would you like to stay for dinner, Leo?" she asks, smiling.

I want to say no, but I can't go back to the Jones' right now. They'd be leaving to the party, and I'd lied that Liam is unwell. I could kick myself about that one. I also don't want to jeopardize having a good relationship with them for the sake of Liam.

"Uh, sure," I say hesitantly, not bothering to hide my confusion.

"We are just having a few friends over this evening. You remember Lucy Smith right? She said she used to go to school with you the last time she was here. Her father works with Trevor," she explains. I immediately regret agreeing to stay for dinner. Lucy Smith and I have a history, we were on and off through high school, mostly because I was never an exclusive boyfriend type. But then again she wasn't an exclusive type of girl either.

"I do." I smile tightly.

Dinner is great. Dawn is expectedly an amazing cook and she cooked up a storm. The men chat animatedly and Trevor is sure to mention to the Smiths that I am now a lawyer. Trevor's wife, Lillian, on the other hand, is sure to mention that she'd seen my mother around town. I recoil at the mention of Lara's name but thank her for sharing that useful bit of information. I notice Lucy gawking at me across the table the entire night, swirling her hair in between her fingers. She holds onto the serving dish for far longer than necessary when passing it to me. I had two beers and two glasses of wine, even though I know that is never a good combination for me. I feel my head spinning but I keep at it. I hate this pretentious dinner party. I shouldn't be here.

Later, I play a few rounds of PlayStation with Liam. I suck at it so bad he flips me off and goes to bed. When did my kid brother start flipping people off? As I walk past the bathroom, I'm unpleasantly surprised to find Lucy perched against the doorframe, a few buttons of her black silk blouse open to reveal a black lace bra. I know what that means and I know I should get the fuck out of here as soon as possible. She beckons me with her finger.

"Where is everyone?" I frown.

"Out on the deck, drinking more," she purrs.

I try to sidestep her, but she places herself in front of me and starts unbuttoning her blouse further, letting it slip off her shoulders.

"We can do this the easy way, Leo, or not, either way we should do this."

She unbuttons her jeans next, and lets them slide down her thighs. I stand staring at her, too drunk to do anything else. I know we can't stay out in the hallway, so I walk into the bathroom despite my conscience screaming at me to run.

She closes the door and stands there in her matching underwear demanding attention. She is undoubtedly a sexy woman. Her black hair falls down to her waist, she has curves in all the right places and she's looking at me like she is already undressing me. I can't help but walk over to her and slip my hands around her waist drawing her to me. She feels familiar. Her lips meet mine, the scent of wine still heavy on her breath. She starts unbuttoning my shirt, trailing kisses down my chest as she does so. She slips her hands around me, digging her long nails into my back. Before I know it, she's on her knees, working my jeans, sliding them off ungraciously. She curls her hands around me. I look down at her and as much as I would like to throw caution to the wind and make her night, something shifts in me and I know I can't let this happen.

"Fuck, Lucy, I don't think this is a good idea," I say, trying to gently pry her off me.

She's unrelenting, but I know I can't do this. I hold her hand and pick her up. As much as I would like to drown my frustrations with Lucy, I know where that would lead. Lucy and I have history and I don't want to distort anything by making out with her now.

"Fuck off," she growls, getting up and hurriedly putting her clothes back on. She turns around and slaps me hard. I deserve it. I let her leave the bathroom. I have to leave, the self-loathing I feel is unbearable. I would deal with Dawn and Trevor another time.

The drive over to the Jones' is a slow one. My phone beeps over and over again, and I know it's Dawn, calling to find out why I left in such a hurry. I can't make myself deal with that now. It is late and I am tired. I can see that they're home because their cars are parked in the driveway. The lights are out so I figure that everyone is asleep. I let myself in and head upstairs, grabbing a towel from the hallway cupboard, slowly making my way to the bathroom. I stand under the shower for what seems like an eternity, allowing the hot spray to wash away the revulsion I feel at myself. I turn the water off and wrap a towel around me, wiping the steam off the mirror. Who am I anymore?

I let myself into my room without a sound and shut the door behind me. I don't notice it when I first walk into the room but as I turn, the moon casts a glow on a lone figure on my bed and I make out the silhouette of Leah. She is sound asleep from what I can tell. Her wild curls are sprawled on my pillow. She looks like a sleeping beauty and my heart skips a beat just watching her. She still has her party dress on. It's a pale pink. The fabric looks soft enough to touch. Wait, why is she in here?

I edge closer and sit on the bed just watching her for

a moment. I move a few stray curls off her face and I can tell she's been crying, her mascara runs down her cheeks and her eyes look puffy, even closed. I feel tightness in my chest. I hate that she was sad on such an important day, knowing it is me who caused it. I did what I thought was right. I didn't want to confuse this whole situation any further.

"Hey," I whisper.

She opens her eyes, slowly adjusting to the dark room. She looks a little startled at first but she lets her eyes roam over my shirtless chest in a way that makes me want to devour her.

"You okay?" I ask, instinctively tucking a curl behind her ear.

"You didn't come," she murmurs.

"I'm sorry, "I try to console her, feeling sick to my stomach with guilt.

She sits up on the bed and then hesitantly climbs into my lap, wrapping her slender arms around my neck, and placing her head against my chest. My heart beats rapidly in my chest as I hold her there for what seems like forever, adjusting so I am sitting more comfortably on the bed. The self-control I am straining to maintain almost waning.

"I'm sorry, baby," I whisper. But her soft breathing tells me she is asleep again.

I want to keep her here with me, keep the scent of

her with me, let it soak into my senses for a while longer, but the realist in me gets up slowly, careful not to wake her again, and I carry her back to her bedroom. As I lay her down and put the covers over her, I do something I'd never done before. I lean down and kiss her forehead. I am losing my mind. I go back to my room, finish changing, and climb into bed. I need sleep. It's been a long fucking night.

I wake up mid-morning. It's Sunday and the Jones' are at church. They often try to recruit me, but that ship had sailed a long time ago. The sun is already high and I could tell it would be one of the warmer days. I have the house to myself and I can make sense of last night. What the heck happened? I enter the hallway and pause. Something is off, a shower, I could hear a shower.

"Fuck," I hiss out loud. Leah is home. I duck into the bathroom, brush my teeth and turn on the shower.

The steam and hot water were inviting. I let myself stay under the spray for longer than necessary then realizing I can't stay there forever I get out. I wrap a towel around my waist, cursing myself for not bringing any clothes with me. I have been accustomed to doing that living with Mrs. J and Leah but I hadn't expected anyone to be home this morning.

I make it to my room just as she's exiting hers. Her white off shoulder dress falls around her slender form, her hair is wet and she looks sexy as…

"Hi, Leo," She smiles at me. The light from the window behind her casts a glow and gives her an ethereal look.

"Hi, Leah," I return barely able to contain my admiration. She flushes when my gaze flits over her.

"I'm really sorry about last night. I don't know what got into me." She looks away nervously.

"It's okay," I assure her, smiling at her reassuringly. "Finding a pretty woman in my bed is hardly any reason to complain." Did I just say that? Shit! A blush spreads across her cheeks and she wraps a curl nervously around her fingers.

"What I mean is, it's really okay," I correct myself.

"Thanks, um, I'll be downstairs. My mom and dad are out for the day," she says, as she heads for the stairs casting me one longing glance. Should I have said more to her? Should I have brought up last night?

I change quickly, kicking myself for saying what I did. I don't want to add to the mix signals I've been throwing her way. I find her at the kitchen table eating toast and tapping away at her phone. *Chatting to Owen no doubt*, I think sarcastically.

"How was your graduation dinner?" I ask.

"Good," she answers not looking at me. She frowns

and sighs continuing the incessant texting.

"We're back to that are we?" I think out loud.

"Back to what exactly, Leo?" she asks through gritted teeth while glaring at me.

"I am talking about this, Leah, these one-word answers and over dramatic silences!" I shout. "I hate this!"

"Well then, why don't you do something about it, Leo, instead of hiding from emotions like a fucking coward," she spits.

She gets up and attempts to leave, but I catch her hand as she passes by me.

"Let go of me," she growls. Her eyes glow like two honey colored flames.

Something about the way she challenges me, how her wet wild hair hangs around her face, stirs something in me. I pull her to me and crash my lips to hers. I kiss her hard and deep and she responds by moaning into my mouth. I pull her closer to me, the sound driving me insane. I hold her between my legs, my hands wrapping around her waist one minute, and exploring the contours of her back the next. I pull away and kiss her gently, letting my tongue taste hers, inhaling her scent and letting my mouth roam down to her smooth neck. My hands move to knead her breasts gently. She wants me, I can feel it. But, I know I have to stop. I stop kissing her but I hold her close to me, stealing a few more minutes of the bliss I feel by having her in my arms, before I know I have to end this.

"I'm sorry, Leah, I can't do this. I shouldn't have started this," I whisper into her ear. "I'm not good for you. I'm not good for anyone." I know that what I'm saying is unfair. I am throwing mixed signals and it isn't right. I can't help it though. When she's near me, I can't think, I just want to feel her closer but I can't deny that I am confused about this whole situation. I don't want to hurt her but it's all I seem to be doing.

She withdraws herself from me, and I can tell that my words have really hurt her. Her eyes are still ablaze. I want to hold her again, but I know better, so I let her leave the kitchen without trying to stop her. She slams the door of her bedroom upstairs, and as the sounds vibrates through the house, I flinch.

She's really too good for me and it's best we both realize that sooner rather than later. A guy like me, with my family history, doesn't deserve a girl like her. She is goodness and purity and I am a walking contradiction. I walk up to my room and change into running clothes, heading out of the front door.

The cool air is welcoming. I need to run, so I do, I run until I can't breathe, until my chest tightens and my muscles protest, until all thoughts of Leah and her beautiful face and how good she feels in my arms are pushed out of my mind if only for a little while.

LEAH

How do you know you're in love? Is it something that happens instantaneously and lies dormant, and then surfaces when the time is right? Is it something that grows and develops over time? Or is it there all the time but changes and takes its true form when the time is right? Whatever it is, I am feeling it.

It's been three months since Leo moved in with us. I am leaving to college in just over three weeks. He is finally moving into his house this weekend. We hadn't talked much since that morning in the kitchen. We tend to avoid each other most of the time. It is easy to do. He started working and is hardly ever around. I suppose that it is for the best. I can't believe that I let myself fall for him the way I did. I stopped denying it. I love Leo Williams, but that feeling is unrequited.

Today is my eighteenth birthday and my parents planned a dinner party at one of my favorite beach restaurants in Camps Bay, Cape Town. It is a bit of a drive from Greyton, but it's worth it if I can spend the evening inhaling the magnificent sea breeze. We drive out to the sea as often as we can as a family but we haven't gone in a while, so this is something I am looking forward to. The sand stretches for miles and the beautiful blue sea kisses the shore and gives out to meet the horizon halfway. There are large rock boulders which the waves crash against and small rock pools where the hermit crabs gather. The whole stretch is full of restaurants and people rollerblading or skating. What I love most is the view of the lighthouse and the oil rigs that sometimes stop over before continuing their journey. It is a sight to behold, especially at night, when their lights hypnotize the watcher.

Kevin will be arriving later this evening. I can't wait to see him. It has been months since we'd last seen my brother. We are going to a nightclub for the after-party. I want to let my hair down and let go of the stresses of the last few months. After looking at myself in the mirror for the umpteenth time, I am pleased enough with my reflection. I am wearing a black ruffled miniskirt and white low-cut chiffon blouse. I let my curls fall loosely around my shoulders and add just a hint of makeup. The white gold hoops and necklace my parents gave me this morning went perfectly with my silver pump heels. Owen is going to be a happy man tonight and who knows how lucky. Leo and I exit our rooms at the same time and he simply stares at me for a while. He has a white button down shirt on, dark jeans that fit him perfectly, and a charcoal blazer. He looks incredible, but I don't say that. I nod at him and he extends a hand.

"Happy Birthday, Leah Jones." He grins, displaying those dimples.

"Thank you," I say tightly, and take his outstretched hand. I feel the heat flowing between our palms and I quickly move, not wanting to let him close again knowing he is just going to reject me later.

We make our way downstairs in silence and I sit in the living room waiting for my parents. Leo thankfully makes himself scarce.

I don't know why I can't seem to get his kisses off my mind. I can't forget how his lips felt against mine and how wonderful he tasted. How his arms felt around me, how I wanted to stay with him forever in that moment. It wasn't just the physical act of kissing him but the fact that I felt it deep within me. A connection. But I can't allow myself to lose my mind over someone who is just not that into me. It's so evident. I can't believe I allowed myself to fall for him.

"Lee-Bear, you look smashing. Happy Birthday, sweetheart," Dad congratulates from behind me.

"Thanks, Dad." I get up to give him a hug.

"Are we all set?" asks Mom, entering the room, looking unbelievable in her simple knee length black dress and shocking blue heels.

Her bag matches her heels and I smile. My mom is still the most beautiful woman I know. She doesn't look her age. Her brown hair is swept up in a curly up style. She is the picture of grace and elegance.

"Leah, you look amazing, come here and get a birthday hug from your mother," she orders, drawing me in. "I'm sure Owen will be pleased," she whispers and winks at me.

My mom really likes Owen. What is there not to like I suppose? I know Bea will argue that, but he has never acted in a way that makes me feel otherwise. Leo on the other hand is everything I have been cautioned against. I hate that my thoughts always go back to him.

"Where's Leo? Leo!" Mom shouts over her shoulder. "Oh my, don't you clean up nicely, young man?" Mom laughs, kissing Leo on the cheek when he joins us.

He laughs and gives her a wink.

"You look beautiful, Mrs. J," he smiles. I can tell he means it. He really does care about my parents. I didn't understand that before, but I do now.

"Thank you, Leo," Mom blushes. "You're embarrassing me."

"And so do you, Leah." he turns to me making my heart skip a beat.

I give him a smile which comes across as a grimace.

His face falls slightly.

"Well, since I'm the only one without a compliment, we'd best leave." Dad laughs.

"You're a stud, Dad." I laugh, looping my hand through his as we all head out of the front door.

The drive to the restaurant is cheery, Mom and Dad sing along to Air Supply and I pull faces at them. Leo doesn't say much to me in the backseat and the atmosphere between the two of us is tense. I look at him and he's staring out of the window, deep in thought. Perfect, I think, another tense evening with Leo. At least Kevin and my friends would be meeting us at the restaurant and that ought to improve my mood and the growing annoyance I feel. My brother's flight is delayed so he would meet us at the restaurant.

Dad pulls into the parking lot at Shoals, my favorite seaside restaurant. The smell of the sea breeze soothes my nerves and instantly lifts my brewing bad mood. I am barely out of the car when Bea tackles me.

"Happy birthday, Leah." She envelops me in a hug and hands me a wrapped gift box and advises me to leave it in the car. I guess that it is yet another pair of shoes. She loves buying me shoes. In fact, the pair I am wearing today was a gift she'd gotten me last Christmas.

"You look stunning." She spins me around.

"So do you, Bea."

She is stunning, and in her silver gray dress that fit her curves perfectly and matching heels, she truly is a vision. She'd transformed her jet-black curls into a long mane with a hair iron and she looks unbelievable. Bea is such a beautiful person, inside-out. It is no wonder that we have been friends for as long as we have. She is the kind of friend who isn't envious. She is comfortable in her own skin which she wears exceptionally well. She has been there for me, cheering me on since kindergarten. She is smart and has a heart of gold.

"Hi, Leo." Bea smiles at him and gives him a wink, which solicits a stunned expression.

"Hi, Beatrice," he says simply.

She scowls at the use of her full name.

We make our way into the restaurant.

The Shoal is set just off the pier and we have a splendid view of the pinkish orange sunset across the Atlantic Ocean. I feel peaceful, like all the turmoil I'd been feeling over the last few months were shedding off me layer by layer. I could breathe again. Our large corner table with white linen and silverware is positioned next to a wall to ceiling patio door, which opens out onto a wooden deck. At night, angel lights transformed the outdoor seating area into a paradise of lights. Even the fact that I had to sit across from Leo wasn't awkward.

This is my special day, and I wouldn't allow anyone, especially Leo, spoil it for me.

"So, this party started without me then?" The familiarity of my brothers booming voice has me instantly shrilling and in tears.

"Kev, you made it!" I shout throwing my arms around him.

"Of course, I made it, wouldn't miss my baby sister's birthday for the world." He hugs me tightly.

"Happy birthday, Princess."

He looks taller, his dark hair is much shorter than I remember, and he's sporting a short beard. There are hugs and kisses all around and Dad orders champagne. I finally feel my spirits lifting. Kevin and Leo do that bro hug and he sits next to Leo. They start talking instantly and are lost to the rest of us until the drinks arrive. Owen arrives, late as usual, and takes a seat next to me after he greets everyone.

"You look amazing, Leah," he whispers into my ear, and I blush immediately. If I hadn't known how uninterested Leo is in me, I would swear he threw daggers Owens way every chance he got. Owen looks amazing in his black button down shirt and gray jeans, his dark hair set perfectly. He laces his fingers through mine and I smile.

"Attention everyone," Dad clinks his glass to break through our chatter, "I would like to propose a toast.

Can we all raise our glasses?" He looks at me, his eyes full of love and pride. I will miss him so much when I leave home. "Our Princess, Happy Birthday. I can't believe my baby girl is eighteen-years-old today, and as you enter this new phase of adulthood all we can wish for you is the best of everything that this life has to offer. You're an incredible, strong-willed and determined young woman. It makes me proud, and I know that you can only succeed in everything you do. I will miss you more than you will know when you're off at college, but I know you're in safe hands…by that, I mean your own, your head's on straight and that's how I know."

My eyes well up and my heart feels like it could burst with the love I feel for my father.

"Thank you, Dad." I get up to hug him and then we all drink to that. There is something so bittersweet about leaving home, especially with the incredible parents I have.

One bottle of champagne turns to three and dinner is incredible. I have the lamb shank with dark chocolate pepper sauce, which is exceptionally tasty. The conversation flows, and having Owen to flirt with and Kevin to bicker with, makes me feel on top of the world and a bit too lightheaded.

Later that night, we wave goodbye to my parents, and the rest of us cram into Owens Mustang and Kevin's rental, heading to the nightclub. Bea's boyfriend, Ethan, meets us at the entrance and we suddenly lose her in the crowd. It is the first time I meet Ethan, but I like him instantly. He is tall, with jet black hair, and gray eyes. They are a beautiful couple together. If she gives him a proper shot that is. My head is still light with the champagne and I appreciate that we instantly find a table in the corner. Kevin and Leo go off to the bar to place our drink orders while Owen and I hang back.

"Hey, Leah, Happy Birthday," Owen leans closer to me and whispers into my ear.

I smile at him and give him a kiss.

"So, you want to dance?" he asks.

"I would love to." I smile at him suggestively as he leads me onto the dance floor.

We dance for a fast song, and the DJ lowers the tempo to something sultrier. I wrap myself around Owen as I glance in Leo's direction where he's now sitting with Kev. He looks at me, amused for a while, but he balls his fists obviously angry, the more Owen caresses me. Why shouldn't Owen caress me, he's my boyfriend? *Fuck you, Leo. Fuck your mixed signals and complicated behavior.*

"I need a drink!" I shout to Owen over the noise.

"Sure, let's get one." He leads me back to the table.

"No, I want one at the bar!" I shout. He nods and

we make our way over to the busy bar. We squeeze our way in and he orders a beer for himself and two shots of tequila for me. We're about to leave the bar when I reach out and take my two shots.

"Whoa, there, maybe you should slow down," he warns.

"It's my birthday, Owen. I want to live a little." I giggle. "Besides, I have never been to a club before and I want to make the most of it, I am sick of small town living, O."

The barman gives me a wink and lines up another four shots of tequila, which he tells me is on him. I down the first three shots, one after the other, no need for the traditional lemon and salt. I am dizzy and it feels good. I push Owen against a barstool and kiss him hard.

"Let's go somewhere," I whisper in his ear. He kisses me back and when we part, he takes my hand and we make our way to a more secluded area of the club, behind the stage.

I'm lost in Owen's kisses and the feel of his hands on my body when a familiar voice interrupts us.

"I think it's home time for you, Leah." Leo's voice drifts from behind me. It sounds like silk and I wonder what it would sound like-no, I can't think like that.

"Hey, man, I'm her boyfriend and I got her here, I'll take her home," Owen interjects, his eyes darkening in anger.

"Where's Kevin?" I cut Owen off, slurring.

"Off mingling, Leah," Leo states, taking hold of my arm.

"I'm not leaving, Leo, why don't you do some fucking mingling yourself and leave me alone? Just scurry on out of here," I defiantly flip him off. He angles his shoulders, preparing for a fight.

"I'll carry you out if I have to, I'll make a scene and I don't give a fuck what you or anyone else thinks," he growls. "I can handle her," Leo adds, addressing Owen who looks like he may throw a punch any second. Leo folds his arms, observing me, begging me to sass him.

"Owen is my *boyfriend* and he will get me home." I smile innocently at Leo. I feel dizzy, really dizzy, so I lean against Owen for support, lacing my hands around him for theatrics.

"Look, I don't have time for this," Leo growls, and the next thing I know, he's bending down and flinging me over his shoulder, carrying me onto the dance floor.

"What the fuck, man—" I hear Owen protesting only to get what I imagine must be Leo's fuck off glare.

Leo stops at our table to collect my handbag and phone.

"Bea," I slur, seeing her at the table on Ethan's lap. "Jerk here wants to take me home." I laugh.

"Maybe that's not such a bad idea." She giggles.

"Traitor," I laugh slanting my eyes and soliciting a laugh from Ethan.

"Can you talk to the boyfriend over there? I'll text Kev. He can catch a ride with you guys. We're leaving," Leo addresses Bea, motioning to where Owen is making his way through the crowd. Bea nods.

"Put me down, Leo, who do you think you are?" I shout at him, getting pissed off now.

"No, Leah, I am not putting you down, you're going home now," he retorts.

"I. Am. Not!" I shout again, slamming my fists against his hard back, and he makes his way toward the exit not pausing or seeming to care about my tantrum.

"Well, well, well, what do we have here, Leo?" says a voice I don't recognize. "I see you have a new pet there, Leo, she's a feisty one." The woman laughs.

"Lucy, I don't have time for this now," Leo tries to brush past her.

"Hi, Lucy," I giggle and slur.

"Weak drunk, isn't she?" Lucy laughs.

"Shut up, Lucy," Leo hisses defensively.

"Whatever." She waves him off. "When you're done baby-sitting, how about you come over to my place Leo, so we can pick up where we left off the other night?" she says teasingly, and by the sound of her voice, I can tell she's edging closer to him.

"I have to go Lucy," I pick up a hint of irritation in his tone.

"Put me down Leo," I shout over the noise. He's been messing around with me and this Lucy woman. He is really a piece of work.

He continues to ignore me and as we near the exit, I know I am not leaving this place with him. I will not be told what to do or treated like a child by this man. I punch his back hard enough that he understands I mean business.

"Put me down right now!" I shout.

He obliges but the look in his eyes silences me.

"You're drunk, your brother asked me to get you home, and so I am doing just that." His jaw twitches.

"I don't feel like leaving," I poke his chest with my finger and glare at him, making sure he understands that this is not up for negotiation.

"Fine, whatever," he grumbles, and stalks over to the table where Bea and Ethan are making out.

Owen approaches, and from the murderous look on his face, I know he is not impressed. "What the fuck was that all about?" he demands, glaring over to where Leo now sits searing.

"Nothing," I brush it off dismissively. "Kevin asked him to look after me so he took it a bit overboard. I want to leave now Owen." I lean into to him playing with a lock of hair. He smiles down at me obviously appeased.

"Your wish is my command, my lady." He bows. He places his hand on the small of my back and leads me to the exit of the club. Outside, the cool air is a welcome change from the stuffy overcrowded nightclub. I am instantly glad we left. We walk to Owen's car and I text Bea to let her know that we're leaving.

"So where to from here?" he asks.

"I want to be anywhere but here." I smirk flirtatiously biting my bottom lip.

"My parents are away this weekend. Would you like to come over?" He grins, sold. I smile up at him. That sounds like just the kind of thing I would like to be doing.

"I'd love to." I get into the car while he holds the door open for me. He starts the car and smiles at me as I rest against the headrest. We are about to take off when Leo opens my door and starts carrying me out.

"You are not leaving with this guy," he snarls. "I will not repeat that, Leah."

Owen is out of the car and between us in an instant.

"I will not tell you again to leave her alone, man," he warns, pushing Leo against the car. The two men face each other off and I hear someone approaching. I glance over to find Kevin.

"What the fuck is going on here?" Kevin shouts, shoving the men apart.

"Owen and I were leaving and your friend here lost it," I inform him smugly, shooting Leo a begrudging glare.

"What? What do you mean you were leaving with him, Leah? That's fucking crazy!" Kevin growls, his irritation evident. "Owen, you should go home, I think it's just a misunderstanding." He calmly extends his hand for a shake. He glares at me and I ignore him.

I don't want Owen to leave, I want to see this night through, but I know there is no way my brother is going to let me leave now.

"I'm sorry," I apologize to Owen, hugging him before he gets into his car. He speeds off.

After saying goodbye to Bea and Ethan, Leo drives us home. I go straight to my room not bothering to say goodnight to either Kevin or Leo. They're both assholes in my book. I mean, who does Leo Williams, think he is, dictating how I spend my time? It's not like I mean anything to him. I quickly text Owen, apologizing to him while stripping out of my clothes. My door creaks open and I freeze because Leo is standing there. I don't move to cover up. Instead I stalk up to him.

"What are you doing here?" I demand.

"I wanted to see that you were alright. You look alright. I'll leave, I'm sorry," he mumbles his eyes darkening as they rake over me.

"You're always so apologetic, Leo, aren't you?" I ask, standing in front of him. I reach for his hands and slowly place them on my ass.

My heart is racing and I can barely breathe, the feel of his hands on me is vexing, but I play it cool and wait for him to make the next move. He pulls me closer to him giving my cheeks a light squeeze.

"You drive me crazy, Leah. I lose my wits around you and I can't afford to do that, not now and not ever," he hisses into my ear and then turns around and leaves me standing there, closing the door behind him.

My emotions are on overdrive as I change and hop into bed. I think about Owen and as much as I like him, I have never felt this way about him. I know that I cannot keep up this farce. I will have to end things sooner rather than later. I close my eyes and I see Leo's face before me. I feel his touch which is burnt on my skin. I know that if he asked me to, I would gladly give him all I am and more.

LEO

I know I want her. I know that what I feel for her is nothing like anything I have ever felt before for anyone. She is weaving her way into my senses and she's drowning me. Leah Jones is so much more powerful than she realizes. She could bring me to my knees. I don't just want her body. I want her heart and soul. I want everything she has to offer. I want to creep into every part of her being, physically, mentally and emotionally. I desire things I have never had with her. I want to experience things I hadn't thought of before. I want to continue feeling things with her and that is what scares me the most. She makes me feel. Something I didn't think was even possible.

Lying on my bed this morning, I think about the night before. She looked so beautiful, too beautiful, standing in front of me exposed, willing. I could've had her, the old me would have, but this version of me who is reserved for her can't think of taking advantage of her like that. Not Leah. I have had my fair share of woman but lately Leah has soiled me for anyone else. I can't think of being with anyone else.

It's 4 a.m., the sun isn't even out yet but I know I need to clear my mind. I put on my running gear and head out. I know where I'm going and head in that direction. The asphalt feels good as my running shoes pound it. I feel the sweat building up and I pick up the pace. My muscles feel free, the fog on my mind starts to lift and I break into a full sprint. It's cool out and the air whips my face as I make my way forward. I can feel my muscles moan and groan, and it motivates me to continue, but I drop the momentum as I near the gate of my new home. I could not believe my luck when the old owner's son decided to put it on sale for next to nothing.

The farm is large, about two thousand five hundred-square feet. The previously old and rundown farm house that sat in the middle of the property has now been transformed into an impressive home. When I moved here a few months ago, I didn't think I would make the progress I did, but Mr. Jones and I made headway relatively quickly. I walk up the wooden staircase onto the newly refurbished front porch but I don't enter the front door, I take a seat on the top stair and look out onto the front lawn. This here is the place I intend to call home. I think about Leah. She looked so peaceful sitting under the oak tree reading a few weeks ago. She is the kind of woman who could bring a man to their knees. I know I am falling for her, I just don't know if it is the right thing for Leah. But I am tired, tired of the back and forth, tired of seeing her with that kid Owen. I could take care of her. I could show her how special she is every fucking day. With that thought, I know what I have to do.

I run back to the Jones,' take a quick shower. I'm in a towel in my room when my door creaks open and I know it's her. "Hey." I smile, letting her know it's okay that she's here.

Her face flushes when she sees me in only a towel. I sit down and pat the bed next to me. She makes her way over to the bed hesitantly.

"I want to apologize for the way I behaved last night, Leo," she whispers. "I didn't mean to make such a scene."

"It's okay, Leah. We were both a little out of hand." I assure her.

"I just didn't understand the way you reacted. I mean, I—" she starts nervously.

Her apology and sincerity in her voice, and the fact that she is so cute when she's nervous, cause me to let my guard down. I pull her toward me and flip us so that she's under me.

"I don't know what's been happening with us either, Leah, but I just know that whatever it is, I want that," I whisper.

She looks at me, stunned. "What changed?" she whispers.

"Everything," I growl protectively. "I don't want you hanging out with that asshole Owen. I don't want to miss the opportunity to know where this could lead. I feel like I'm losing my mind and if I don't have you…" I touch my forehead to hers. "I just have to have you, you're mine," I confess as calmly as I can muster.

"How do I know you're not going to go cold turkey on me again. Besides, I'm leaving to college in a few weeks, Leo, what can come of this? You're moving this weekend and my family, Kevin, they will never understand this, whatever this thing is between us," she says worriedly.

"I don't know, I don't have any answers, but I'm hoping we'll figure it out, together," I say letting my hands stroke her face. She is mine. I could feel her resistance yielding.

"We can't tell them just yet," she states. "You're a family friend, you've been living here, they'll think the worst," she rambles.

"We don't have to do anything rash. Not until we figure this all out," I say, leaning in closer to her. I kiss her forehead gently. *You've got to be gentle with her*, my conscience whispers.

I let my lips trail kisses from her forehead, to her cheeks, and then our lips meet, and I kiss her with more force that I intend. My knees settle between her thighs and she moans. It's such a beautiful sound, but something that can drive me insane if I'm not careful.

"You're so beautiful, Leah Jones." I kiss her with all the pent up need and anguish I feel. I kiss her with the desire that I know will set our world off kilter. I want her now, and I need to get lost in her. I don't care that we are just starting this thing.

"I've wanted you for so long, it's all I've been thinking about since the first time you kissed me," she whispers, her hands tangling in my hair, begging me to take her, but I drag myself back to reality. This is Leah, and she matters too damn much.

"I can't, Leah, not now, I want you with everything in me but I can't, it's too soon," I whisper.

She lifts her hips to meet my hard on, giggling and I almost cave.

"You'll be the death of me, Leah Jones." I stand up quickly securing my towel around my waist.

She gets up, pouting. She kisses my cheek and leaves the room with a wink and I can't for the life of me believe what just happened.

I just asked Leah Jones to be mine and she agreed.

What the fuck has gotten into me? I shake my head and get dressed.

"So what's really the plan with this place, Leo?" she asks, walking around the kitchen while I whip us up some ham and cheese sandwiches.

"What do you mean?" I ask her.

"I mean, I know you're ambitious and you want to do big things, somehow I don't see Greyton doing all that for you." She takes a seat at the island.

I moved into my house three weeks ago and these have been the best weeks of my life.

I smile at her, amazed at how well she knows me in such a short time. I walk over to the kitchen island and spin her toward me.

"You know me a bit too well, Ms. Jones," I kiss her lightly. She wraps her arms around my neck and I take in her amazing scent.

"Truthfully, Leah," I back up to look into her eyes, "I want to maybe rent this place out for the holidays, the town is slowly growing and this place would make an amazing guesthouse for tourists."

She considers me.

"But, you're right, once, I've got my experience at the firm, I want to move to the city, get a full-time job there, and become filthy rich." I tickle her.

"Will you have a Rolls-Royce?" She giggles.

"Nah, I'm a Porsche guy, it'll pick up more chicks."

She gasps and swats me playfully. "You know, Leo, I don't doubt you can do all of that and more."

I pull her close to me and kiss her forehead. Leah has come to mean so much to me in such a short time. I don't know how I'll be able to let her go, or even if I want to.

Leah is leaving for college in two weeks. Things between us are becoming more intense in a short space of time. What we share makes me realize that Leah and I are closer than we care to admit. We are definitely closer than I have ever been with any other woman. I am starting to understand the difference between the real thing and everything else. Leah is different. She's laid back, maybe immature at times, but responsible, in just the right proportions. She is silly enough to have pillow fights with but we can sit and talk about different things for hours, cars, poetry, space, procreation, and the meaning of life. She doesn't just listen to my words, she listens to my heart and soul.

I learned things about Leah I hadn't known before, like that no matter what she ended up majoring in, which she hoped would be English literature. She wants to help people in some way and make a difference in their lives. She wants to have a big family and chase her kids around the garden playing hide and seek. She also dreams of writing books filled with romance and tragedy.

I love talking to her, I love getting to know her, and in time, I find myself opening up to her in ways I have never allowed myself to with anyone else. I speak to her openly about my fascination with foreign language movies, like *Vampyr* and the *Grand Illusion* from the 1930's. We spent hours listening to my collection of 40's jazz music. She often asks me to read to her out loud, and although it feels strange at first, I grew to enjoy those moments between us. We spent countless nights, her perched between my legs, listening to me read from *The Great Gatsby*, just the two us, sharing and listening.

She didn't realize the effect she had on me and if she did, she is good at hiding it. Leah is effortlessly beautiful which makes her hard to resist but I do, with great difficult.

She is perfection, but I didn't want to rush things, no matter how difficult it is to say no to her when she comes onto me. She isn't just any woman, she is Leah, and when I did have her, it would be special. Something she will never be able to forget.

We're sitting under the shade of the large oak tree in my front garden. It's one of our favorite places, it's quiet here and we can think and talk about what's on our minds. We don't have to pretend here. It's just us. I moved into my house a few days ago and I already felt settled. Still, as happy as I am for the progress I've made, my heart is heavy at the thought of her leaving. I hadn't realized I am so far away in thought until she snaps her fingers in front of my face.

"Earth to Leo. What's on your mind, handsome?" Her eyes meet mine and I smile at the wonder in them. With Leah, I see myself as more than just Leo, the young man with a bad family history trying to establish himself in society. I feel like the greatest human being on the planet. She looks at me that way and I never want that to change.

She's lying with her head in my lap and I stroke her curls with my fingers, loving the feel of the softness. I bend down and kiss her forehead. It is my way of showing her I cherish her.

"It's nothing, babe." I smile down at her.

"It can't be nothing if you're so far away in thought,"

I lean down and kiss her forehead again, choosing my words carefully. "In a few weeks, you'll be gone and I won't be able to hold you like this or see you all the time. I'll miss you." I stroke her cheek and she leans into my hand.

"I know. I'll miss you too, Leo."

"Stay, go to college closer to home," I blurt out without thinking, bringing my lips down to meet hers.

She looks at me, her eyes welling up and I know it breaks her heart to hear that. "I love you, Leo." It's the first time she says those three words and I know she means it. Three simple words filled with so much promise.

"And I love you, Leah. I never knew I was capable of love until you."

Hearing me say those words out loud is believable. I do love her, in every sense of the word.

"I love you so much, but I can't stay here. I need to leave. I need to spread my wings outside of this town," she says softly. "We will still see each other, Leo, just not as often as this."

I know she's right, but the thought of losing her is crippling. I kiss her and drop the topic feeling appalled at my own selfishness. I lean back against our tree and watch the clouds drift above me through the branches, an analogy for her drifting away from me.

"Tell me about what it was like growing up, about your dad," she prompts.

It's not something I talk about, but I want to talk about it with her. Kevin knew a lot about what I'm about to say, but telling it to Leah feels different.

"I don't remember my dad too well. I was very little

when he died. But I do know that when he did, my life changed. My mother changed. Nothing was the way it used to be. I went from being the center of her universe to no one." Leah takes my hand in hers and holds it over her chest.

"My mother treated me like I was nothing, like I was not even worth the cheap cologne her men wore. Kevin often asks me whether I will ever talk to her again, and honestly, I don't know. Respect is earned, Leah, and it's a two-way street. My mother never earned mine and she never gave me any. I had to grow up too soon and take care of Liam. In the process, I forgot what it was like to be a child until I met Kevin. I had to endure things no child ever should and it made me hard and unfeeling for a long time. It made me angry, and above all, it made me believe the things she told me, that maybe I was worthless." I looked at her, waiting for her to say something.

"You are worth it, Leo." She reaches up to caress my cheek.

Those simple words, spoken by the woman I love, make everything I have ever been through in my life seem insignificant. I believe her and I finally, believe I am valuable despite the opinion of my mother and everyone else in this town. I'm also certain that I will never love another woman the way I love this beautiful woman.

"Will you have dinner with me?" I ask her, my eyes pleading with her to say yes.

She smiles and that's my answer.

I watch her at the kitchen table, a glass of sweet white wine in hand, as she looks outside the glass doors leading onto the porch, at the setting sun. Her hair is loose and wild, just the way I like it, and she has on a blue summer dress.

"I love this kitchen, Leo, I love the view of the trees and the lake you have." She gets up, walks over to the door, and opens it, stepping onto the porch.

I am putting the finishing touches on the green salad. A combination of lettuce, tomatoes, cucumber, feta cheese, and peppers. The steaks are already grilling outside and I will check them in a few seconds to make sure they're medium well, just the way we both like it.

I've set the table out on the back porch earlier. I am not any good at all this, but Leah made me better at a lot of things. I love how being with her makes me believe that I can be so much more. I know that no matter how far apart we are, I would do anything to see her, even if it means driving out to her every other weekend.

I place the salad and wine on the table and walk over

to wrap my arms around her waist. She leans into me and it's amazing how perfectly she fits there.

"Thank you for this."

I nuzzle into her neck, causing her to giggle. "I've got to check those steaks," I whisper against her neck, loving the goosebumps that form there when I do.

I lay the steaks on the plates and she joins me. I pour her more wine and we eat in a comfortable silence.

Sometimes, words aren't necessary. Contentment is felt in the depths of the soul.

Leah insists on cleaning up afterwards, and I let her, knowing that is one argument I won't win. I pour her more wine and she starts singing off key to a song on the radio. I love this woman. I know it. I feel it. I walk over to her and take her in my arms, gently swaying with her. I love the feel of her in my arms and I let myself trail tiny kisses from her lips to her ears and back again. Her breath hitches and I feel like if I don't feel her close to me tonight, I never will. I start to unzip her pretty blue dress, never taking my eyes off her. I allow my fingers to feel her smooth skin as I slide her dress gently off her body. She continues to sing as I start to kiss my way from her neck to her collarbone, my eyes meeting hers and they're like two honey orbs. I spin her around and then wrap my arms around her.

"I want to take you upstairs," I whisper.

"What took you so long, Leo Williams?" She smiles,

reaching up to run her fingers through my hair. She looks at me like I am her world and she offers up her heart and soul for me to take. I don't wait another minute before I carry her upstairs, where I place her on my bed.

She's serious, she's nervous, and it's the most beautiful combination I've ever known. Her eyes meet mine in the near dark, and at that moment, I decide that she is the most beautiful woman I have ever laid my eyes on. She is like the full moon on a dark night, she lights up my world. I undress slowly and hover over her, making sure not to put my weight on her.

"You don't have to do this now," I whisper placing my forehead against hers.

"I want to," she wraps her legs around my waist, her hands in my hair.

I slowly remove her white lace underwear, unwrapping her like my favorite gift on Christmas morning.

"You're everything to me, Leah Jones, everything."

I make love to her slowly, enjoying every minute, worshiping every part of her body, etching her into my memory. Being with her is like nothing I have ever experienced before. This is not my first time with a woman, but it felt like it. I connected with her heart and soul, and as she gave herself to me, I promise to keep her safe. I promise her my own heart and soul, and when she falls asleep in my arms, I listen to the sound of her breathing, unable to believe that she is mine.

When I drop her off at her house the next morning, her father isn't at all impressed. The Jones family like me enough as Kevin's friend and to help me out and let me stay in their house when I needed to, but lately when it comes to hanging out with their baby girl, it doesn't seem like they are as friendly as they used to be, especially her father. He sees me as I am: trouble for his daughter. Someone who can distract her enough to miss a chance with her dreams. I don't blame him. I would not be happy if my little girl spent the night with a guy like me. I am not a preppy kid, I grew up as the troublemaker, and even though I have changed and grown up, some things never completely change.

I watch as Leah waves goodbye under her father's disapproving gaze, and I nod curtly before driving to visit Liam.

The kid always lifts my mood, but today even he doesn't help. I'm distracted. We play chess and he beats me. Dawn is in a foul mood and her mood doesn't help my situation either. So I just leave. It was rude of me to leave her dinner party without thanking the host and hostess.

An uneasiness claws my insides, so I text Leah asking if she'd like to do anything tonight, but her reply is distant and she doesn't want to go out with me. She says her parents think that we should take a little break until she leaves so they can spend some time with her, but I can see the underlying message, they are hoping that she'll forget me. She promises that that won't happen and she'll see me tomorrow.

I'm frustrated, angry, and bitter. I go to a pub and drink more than I should. I don't text Leah again. I know she is not at fault, but I am angry with her too.

The pub is busy, and everyone seems to be climbing over each other to get a drink. I get a stool in the furthest corner and order a whiskey. I am not a drinker. I have never been one since high school but tonight is an exception. My phone buzzes and I see that it's Leah. I ignore the call and let it go to voicemail.

She tries to call me a few times, but after a few more drinks, I know I'm not in the right frame of mind to speak to her. I need to clear my head so I drink some more.

I allow the harshness of the strong stuff burn my throat and senses. I have to do something. I can't lose her. But what do I do? Both our lives are just beginning. We both deserve a chance at something more, something bigger. Isn't that what I planned for my life all along?

I drink until the atmosphere in the pub is just a blur.

Someone sits next to me and I can't make out much

about his features. He's buying himself a gin and tonic. He greets me and I greet him back. I tell them about Leah and that she'll be leaving me in a few days. I drink until everything is a blur and I remember that this is just the kind of thing I promised never to do. *I promised I would never be like her, drowning her problems with a bottle.* I pay my bill, barely able to walk, and I tell myself that I will never drink again because this is the kind of lack of control that destroys people.

I wake up the next morning to incessant knocking at the front door and a killer headache. For a moment, I don't know where I am but the light from the lace curtain window, which almost blinds me, tells me I'm at home. I get up slowly and reach for the bottle of water on my bedside table. It's warm. I force it down and get up. Why the fuck am I so dizzy? I make my way into the living room and realize I should have put on some pants. I hear the shower down the hallway and find that to be odd. I must be hearing things.

The knocking persists.

"I'm coming!" I shout and just as I swing the door open to greet whoever is there, Lucy exits my bathroom in only a bath towel.

"Morning, sunshine," she hums.

"What the fuck?" I bark, and it is then that I notice

Leah standing at the door. She looks between Lucy and me, the disbelief apparent on her face. She shakes her head and starts to back away.

"Leah," I all but whisper her name. "Wait!" I shout, but she's already walking away quickly.

"No, Leo, don't say anything!" she shouts.

Pants, I need pants. I run into my bedroom and grab the first pair I can reach. I catch up to her as she's getting into her dad's car.

"Baby, please," I beg as she locks the doors.

She's crying and it hurts to see it. To think I caused it. She puts the car into drive without even looking at me and she pulls off. She doesn't stop, she runs a red light trying to get away from me and I stand there feeling like the total fuck up I have always been. The heavens open and before I know it, I'm soaked through. Without thinking, with just my pants on, shoeless and shirtless, I break into a run all the way to her house hoping I am not too late. She has to understand. I have to explain. The night before hits me like a truck. Nothing happened. I wouldn't do that to her, she has to see that. I can't lose her. I won't.

2016

He realized early on,
That there was a fire within her,
It could not be tamed,
It could not be extinguished,
He understood,
and fanned her flames.
- Jo-Anne Joseph

LEO

I've never given much thought to dying, I figured it would happen at some point, but when it did I would be much older and ready for it. That's the thing about life. Those things you don't consider to be important are the things that sometimes creep up on you unannounced. It's the things you should have focused on or paid just a little bit more attention to, that matter.

I didn't want to imagine gradually ceasing to exist. I didn't want to imagine slipping into nothingness. That isn't how things were supposed to be for me. I am forty-years-old. I didn't look it, and I sure as hell didn't feel it. I've made something of myself. Leo Williams, the hot shot commercial lawyer. I have graced the covers of business magazines and I've been in the news. My job required precision, so how is it that I completely missed the plot on this one? I've spent a lot of time focusing on my work and very little time focusing on much else, including myself.

My phone rings and I walk to my large mahogany desk which cost me a fortune to import. I admit I have become somewhat high maintenance. I don't spend enough time doing anything that matters anymore and sometimes I feel like I've lost a great big chunk of my soul. I place the sheet of paper I've been holding into the top drawer and I pick up the receiver. The jolly voice of my best friend awaits me on the other side. "Jones, to what do I owe this pleasure?" I joke.

"Hey man, I just wanted to remind you that Tania and I will be joining you for dinner tonight." My best friend's voice is always so full of humor. He reminds of who I used to be.

I smile quietly and want to take a dig at him about Tania being a special one for Kev to be bringing her over, but think otherwise.

"Of course, man, I am practically out of the door." I laugh.

"Great, see you tonight, Leo."

"See you later, Kev." I end the call.

I hadn't seen my best friend in two years. He was assigned to a project in London for two years and since his return, between our schedules there didn't seem to be enough time. Kevin Jones is a brilliant man. This visit was long overdue. I need to unwind. I am too young for all this. I straighten my desk, tell my personal assistant I am leaving, and do something I don't often do, I leave the office before dark.

I get home early, shower and change into chinos and a light blue button down shirt. Walking downstairs, I marvel at the extravagance of my home. I have never interested in material things when I was younger, having grown up as a young man of limited means. But at the first taste of luxury, I knew I had to surround myself in it.

The two sitting areas each boast plush couches and rugs. The one with the view of the mountain range has a large fireplace with a towering bookshelf, whilst the other one, the larger of the two, has a selection of paintings on the walls by local artists. The dining area is large and airy with glass doors that lead out to a wooden deck and heated pool. I can see my housekeeper Jana, fussing around in there despite the fact that she always has everything in order hours before. I shake my head and go to greet her.

"Hi, Mr. Williams." Jana smiles at me widely.

"This is great, Jana," I compliment her.

"Thank you so much." She smiles proudly, and starts rattling off about the theme and menu.

I try to listen as I always do, but I am thankfully saved by the bell.

"I'll get that." She turns to leave.

I follow close behind and enter the foyer to find Kevin and a hot little redhead I have thankfully never met or slept with before, shrugging out of their coats.

"Kev." I grab my friend in a bear hug.

"Leo." He pats me on the back.

"Good to see you." I grin. I move my attention to my other guest.

"This is Tania." Kevin smiles at the pretty red and I take her hand in mine and plant an overzealous kiss on it while winking at her. Kev rolls his eyes and laughs.

"It's so good to have you both here."

"Thanks for having us." Tania blushes.

Jana comes forward with welcome drinks. Kevin and I both decline and I ask her to give Tania the tour. I lead Kevin into the bar for some real drinks.

"Beer or stronger?" I ask.

"Stronger." Kev laughs.

"Man, it's been so long."

"I know, bro, so much has been going on," he responds. He relaxes on one of the leather high back armchairs.

"So what is the real order of business before we get this party started?" I look at him suspiciously.

He laughs. It's a hearty laugh that reminds me of his dad, his eyes light up and they remind me of a time long passed and someone else with a similar pair.

"Just like you to cut to the chase." He smirks. I nod and pass him bourbon.

"I'm getting married, bro!" I can't say I'm surprised.

We're both getting older.

"That's awesome. When did this all happen?" I ask, coming forward to slap him on the shoulder good-naturedly.

"I met Tania about a year and a half ago back in London and we just clicked, she's not like anyone else I've ever dated, she's different, real, and I knew that I needed more of that in my life, so three months ago, I popped the question," he says.

The content expression on his face is comforting. I doubt I will be that excited about proposing to a woman.

"So this visit is to actually invite me for the wedding isn't it?" I laugh.

"It's actually to ask you to be my best man," he corrects more seriously. "I wouldn't want anyone else standing by my side when I marry the woman of my dreams, you'll have my back, right, man?" he asks.

"Yes," I answer my friend, as there is no thought necessary.

This is my best friend and brother. He stands up and we embrace and move away awkwardly as men usually do.

"So, when is the big day?" I question, refilling our glasses.

"Next month." He beams.

"You don't waste any time, do you?" I laugh almost

spluttering my drink.

Dinner is pleasant and as I sit across the room looking at my friend, the joy he radiates is infectious. I wonder what it must be like to feel that kind of love and that kind of hope for a future with a woman you truly love.

"You're still working yourself to the bone?" he asks matter-of-factly.

I frown at my friend, knowing this would be a topic of discussion.

"The whole business tycoon thing has never been you, Leo, you've always wanted to help kids, practice family law, and make sure kids didn't get the bad end of the stick," he continues.

"I know, Kev. I thought about that today." I smile at my friend and marvel at how he sometimes knows me so well. Even time and distance hasn't changed that. "I just might give it some thought." We raise our glasses to that.

Later that evening, when they'd left, I leave too, to spend a few hours with Megan, my lady of convenience, and as she bucks and moans beneath me, I think back to a time when I did love a woman as intensely as Kevin loves Tania, where she and my dreams were intertwined, and the pain that love eventually caused me. I bury my head in Megan's hair and I pretend I am not really here, in this room, in this woman I barely know or understand. I imagine instead, sitting in a small room on a single bed having a pillow fight with a young woman. I hit her on the back with a big stuffy pillow and she keels forward onto the bed laughing only to get back up again and drag me back to her. I kiss her deeply and I want to stay in that room forever.

Megan moans, cutting through my thoughts, and I lose myself in her as we reach climax. I don't sleep over, instead I gather my things and leave and later, when I am in my own bed and the sleep evades me yet again, I get up and go to my study to conceal myself in work, my saving grace. The case I am working on is intense and it is just what I need to get my mind off everything. This is after all, what I should be focusing on.

LEAH

Sitting in my small office, I await the arrival of my last client for the day. My receptionist had taken the afternoon off. I left the door to the front office ajar so I could hear Alice Peters and her five-year-old daughter Diana when they arrive. I love my work as a private Speech and Language therapist, it is a rewarding career, not in the monetary sense, but in so many other ways, and I wouldn't trade for the world.

I set my practice up four years ago and before that I worked at the local hospital where the hours were longer and I was bound by all kinds of rules and regulations about treatment regimens, which I just didn't agree with. It was a long shot going out on my own but I took the chance and I was fortunate that most of my clients left with me. I enjoy what I do and the small corner office with a park view. Even when it is cloudy my office always finds the light. When it rains, it is a view from a postcard between the large curtains from my floor to ceiling windows. But my favorite is the sunny days when the warm glow compliments the simple décor of my office. My thank you wall is my pride and joy. It is filled with paintings, pictures, and drawings from my younger patients.

Diana bursts through my door before her mother, carrying her signature brown bear, and knocks over some magazines in a stand. She plops down on a couch and I get up to go over and kneel down in front of her

"Hey, Di and Buttons, how are the two of you doing today?" I ask, giving them each a handshake.

Alice Peters follows, clearly exasperated, and throws me an apologetic look while picking up the magazines which have fallen. I wave it off and I smile at her.

"Hi, Alice," she almost greets back until Di interrupts.

"We are ok," Di beams.

Alice and I both clap our hands because she uttered that line without a stutter. I've been working with Diana for over year now and at first her progress was very slow but the developments I've seen in the last three months have been magnificent.

"Well done, Di, I can tell you've been practicing your exercises everyday like a good girl," I smile.

"Yes, Miss, Le-ah, I am," she pronounces the words carefully.

I give her a high five. We go through our routine

exercises, flashcards, front hops which are one of her favorite exercises where she does frog hops to six lily pads reading the words on it, and gets rewarded with a sweet. When she's ready to leave an hour later I am more positive than ever. I love when my patient leaves with a sense of accomplishment. It is incredible because every time a client progresses, so do I.

"You're amazing with kids," Alice states as she gets ready to leave and I feel my insides clench.

"Thank you," I smile at her and watch them leave.

Children are a sore topic for me. After eleven years of marriage, Owen and I were still not parents. Owen Devlin and I had got back together soon after I graduated and we've been together ever since. He tried to make me happy, as happy as he knows how. I remember early on in our marriage when we used to laugh about everything. He has never been the boy next door, but I do love Owen. He is smart, handsome and he's nothing like he used to be. But lately I can't help but feel a growing rift between us. It's hard to explain sometimes, I just feel it. It eats at me and makes me angry. We argue all the time and he's easily infuriated by simple things. It doesn't help that he is away for work about a week every month, sometimes more.

"O," I shout, when I enter our house an hour later.

"In here," he shouts from the living room.

"Is that?" I almost shriek.

"You bet it is." I run over to where he stands installing our new flat screen TV.

"Wow, it's epic." I laugh, nearly smashing into the television and him.

"Easy, babe, I can't live another week without *Desperate Housewives.*"

I laugh at that and give him a kiss on the cheek. "Can we afford it, though?" I ask tentatively.

"Why would you even ask that, of course we can?" he hisses.

I'm startled at his tone but try to ignore it.

"I'm going to start dinner," I say as I leave the room. I think about Owen's reaction as I make my way down the hallways, but decide that it is not worth overthinking anything he says or does these days. He'll be himself in a few minutes.

I walk into the kitchen, and I am startled at the sight of my brother at the kitchen island.

"You jerk!" I shout at him, exasperated. "Owen!" I shout and I hear my husband laugh in the living room.

"You didn't think he could install that TV all on his own, did you?" Kevin laughs and I poke at his chest teasingly.

"When did you get here? Oh my, I haven't even prepared supper," I say.

"Relax, all done, Owen ordered in." Kev grins, giving me a spin. It feels so good to see my brother again.

He's still as playful as ever.

"You're too thin, Leah," he announces after setting me on my feet.

"Shut up." I laugh and swat him. I can't believe my brother is here in my kitchen. No one told me he was coming. He is indeed a sight for sore eyes. I hug him one more time.

"Hi," says a small voice from behind me.

I turn around to find a pretty redhead walking up to us.

"Tania!" I can't hold my excitement and pull her into a hug. Mom called me weeks ago about Kev's new girlfriend and I decide that she is far prettier than her Facebook profile picture.

"It's so lovely to finally meet you, wow, this really is a surprise, a great one," I say taking Kev's hand in mine. "And my husband decides to order in!" I yell.

"Oh, that is nonsense, takeout is perfect." Tania smiles.

Kevin comes around us and slides his arms over our shoulders, directing us to the living room. "We get to catch up more," he says, kissing my cheek.

Our Chinese food arrives a few minutes later and we chat and eat, catching up on my brother's time overseas. He regales us with the tale of his and Tania's whirlwind romance and finally breaks the news of their proposal to which I shriek and have the men covering their ears. We crack open some champagne to celebrate and laugh till late in the evening. I am surprised to hear that the wedding would be held next month but also glad that my brother has found someone special after all this time. Tania seems like a wonderful person and there is no doubt that she makes my brother happy. I look across at Owen and I can't help but wonder if we'll ever be okay again, like we used to be. Tania and Kevin take the guest bedroom and I say good night, making my way to my bedroom. I hear their laughs as I make my way down the hallway and smile.

I decide that a shower is well deserved. I step into the hot spray and let it loosen my tight muscles. I'm surprised when I feel Owen's hands on my shoulders, gently kneading the tension away, and I smile despite my reservations. I lean into him and he wraps his arms around my waist.

"I missed you," he whispers, trailing kisses from my earlobe to my neck. My heart rate picks up and as much as I want to step away, I don't. I let him touch me. I let him take me, fiercely, each of us giving as much as we possibly can. On the outside, our life looks wonderful, but on the inside, it couldn't be further from the truth. Later that night as I drift off to sleep, with Owen snoring gently beside me, his hands across my middle, I wonder what this night means for us, or if it means anything at all.

LEO

Being the best man is more work than I anticipated. A few days ago, Tania presented me with a checklist, an actual checklist for goodness sakes. It details every last thing I should do and a whole other list of don't-do's. Kevin sure initiated her well on the life and times of Leo Williams because I saw "No Strippers," about four times on the list of don'ts.

Women!

Over the course of the last few days, between work and interviews for yet another business piece for *Forbes*, I have played the role of trusted advisor, confidant, planner, and even chauffeur to my best friend. Isn't it enough that I've been there for him through thick and thin including high school? Actually, we were there for each other. I got a few punches thrown my way for him and he got me out of a lot of sticky situations with his charm and good reputation.

I complain to him every chance I get, but in all hon-esty, this couldn't have come at a better time. I can do something other than bury myself in work and I don't have to think about the document sitting in the top drawer of my office desk. It calls to me, but I refuse to answer. I walk over to the large windows overlooking the park. It's a dull day in Cape Town but my spirits are high, I feel better than I have in months. I feel deeply honored that after all these years Kevin would want me by his side on the most important day of his life.

Kevin has been in my corner during my darkest times, he always seemed to know me better than I knew myself. Growing up, we were an unlikely pair, he was a good kid, parents who doted on him and did their best to make sure he had the right opportunities. I was trouble, always have been with no real adult support growing up. I haven't spoken to my mother in years but my brother has. She may be trying to get herself together but she will always be a low life drunk to me, a drunk who abandoned her children when they needed her the most and I am still completely uninterested in her.

I look down at the checklist and decide that it's time to make an appointment for suit fittings. Now there is something I am used to. It might in fact be the most enjoyable part of this whole traumatic affair. I pick up my mobile and dial Dave and Sons, my tailors. They pick up on the second ring.

"Dave and Sons, good evening," the stoic voice of Tara, the front store assistant, greets me.

"Tara, it's Leo Williams, is Dave still in?"

"Mr. Williams, good evening, sir, I'll put you straight through. "

The perks of being me, I think to myself.

"Leo," Dave greets me cheerfully. "To what do I owe this pleasure, you aren't thinking of a new collection already, are you?"

I laugh at that. "No, Dave, not yet anyway, actually I have a favor to ask,"

"Ask away," he responds.

"My best friend is getting married in a month and I'd like to make an appointment for suit fittings for the wedding party. You think you can fit us in?" I know the answer but ask him anyway.

"I'm sure I can, how does next week Friday sound?" Dave asks.

"That is perfect. We can definitely do that. I guess that's off my to-do list now." I laugh.

"Good luck, Leo, this wedding business is a nightmare and at such short notice." He chuckles.

"Thanks, Dave." I hang up. I'm going to need all the luck I can get. He is right, it is a nightmare.

I never did the wedding thing or saw the value in it. No one I met was ever good enough, I guess I constantly measured them against a ghost. What did I expect? I doubted that I would ever do it anyway. I open my top drawer and look at the manila envelope staring back at me. I touch it gently as if it would burn me if I held it. I stand up and make my way out of the office.

My house is quiet when I arrive home and I remember that my housekeeper is visiting with her mother. I feel like I can breathe. I hate being smothered. Jana has taken on the role of a mother figure and it's exhausting at times. Dale checks in with her at least once a week. I love my aunt, but she's constantly putting ideas into Jana's head that I need to be babied. I don't.

I pour myself a glass of sherry and go to my den. I consider calling Liam but realize that that it's far too late. He always has a long day and values his sleep. Liam and I remain close. We talk as much as we can. He is touring Spain now, walking the Camino de Santiago, the anthropologist in him. I can't wait for Christmas, he'll be home and we can finally catch up. In some ways, my brother is so much like me it's scary. He's non-committal, evasive but with the great exception that from an early age he has been in search of himself, non-destructively. He's fascinated with human nature. Liam has found a way to forgive our mother and they've even been talking from time to time, and as much as I wish it wasn't the case, I respect that. My mother wants to speak to me but there isn't much to say. I send her a check regularly and that's about all I can manage. I heard she left Lawn and is on her own, trying to get her shit together. Not that I care. I stopped caring a long time ago.

I text Kev and tell him about our first suit fitting appointment and I immediately receive a response back from Tania thanking me for taking this so seriously. I wonder what it must be like to trust someone the way those two do and to be so inseparable. And then I remember Leah. There was no one after Leah, not in the same way. It started and ended with her. I hadn't thought of her in years. I didn't want to. I never looked her up or tried to get in contact with her. Kevin mentioned once that she'd gotten married and settled down, married that piece of shit Owen, I never liked the guy. There was just something off about him.

With the wedding looming I know I will have to see Leah again, but I remind myself that I shouldn't really bother myself with that. That part of my life is over, and as much as I may have loved her once, it is all in the past. She is just a woman after all, and like all woman, she shouldn't be deified.

LEAH

My brother is getting married. When we were younger, I always figured he would marry first and I would follow, and now here I am married for a solid eleven years and my older brother is only just taking his first steps toward it. It's pouring out and I am driving to our family home in Greyton where our parents are throwing Kevin an engagement party. I wish the weather had held out for just a little while, it's an hour and a half long drive and the constant rain and wind makes it difficult for me to see more than a few feet in front of me. I even wish Owen were here, but he's busy on a critical project, yet again, so he can't join us. I'm not surprised. This is the norm. There is always something more important for Owen to be doing.

I haven't been to my parents' home in three months and that is excessively long for me. I miss the smell and especially the taste of home. My mother is still a superb cook and my meager attempts can't compare.

I turn up the radio and some new pop song is on, it's a good tune so I leave it on. I'm thirty-four-years old so my taste in music has significantly evolved. I pick up speed a little but reduce it as a road closure sign becomes visible. "Shit." I bang the steering wheel.

The detour route will take me an extra half hour and I know I will need to stop and fill gas for that. I see a garage sign up ahead and decide I may need to stop there and that's when I feel it, a slight vibration at first but it rapidly increases and my car starts swerving to the left. I don't have to be a rocket scientist to know it's a blowout. My heart is in my mouth but I know I have to remain calm. I remember reading about blow outs somewhere. I hold the steering wheel firmly hoping the car will slow down by itself. I don't brake but drop a gear and keep the steering wheel in a straight line, thanking my lucky stars when my car starts to drop speed, but not gentle enough as before I know it, I'm heading straight for a concrete barrier.

The rain is beating down harder and I try to breathe but the panic I'm feeling is overwhelming, the impact shakes me up pretty badly and I slump over on my steering wheel. My hands are shaking uncontrollably and I can't see clearly, and after a moment, everything just seems to fade to black.

I didn't know how long I'd been out but an oddly familiar voice brings me back to the present. It's cold and my head hurts a bit.

"Lady," I make out the exasperated male voice. "Open the window," the words flow in and out of my consciousness.

I can hear the rain beating down harder on the car roof. I know I need to get up but I can't. My head feels heavy and all I want to do is sleep.

"Can you hear me?" the voice seeps into my consciousness again.

I nod but I don't know if my head is moving or not, I can't breathe and my head hurts.

"Lady," he repeats, and I finally open my eyes. Everything is slightly blurry and there is a throbbing pain behind my eyes. I am thankfully still in my car. The rain pelts down heavily. A black SUV is parked in front of me, and as I slowly turn my head to the side, I see that someone is indeed knocking at my passenger window. I click unlock and a man opens the passenger door.

"Are you okay?" he questions.

I lean back against the headrest, spent, and offer a gentle nod.

"The paramedics are on the way," he says. "I'm not sure how long they'll be, we're kind of in the middle of nowhere."

"No, I have to be somewhere," I object in barely a whisper, leaning on the steering wheel again.

"You need to be in a hospital lady, are you hurt?" he

asks, his irritation growing, and even in my exhausted state, I wonder what his deal is.

"No, no I'm okay." I pick my head up and it feels heavy, I must have bumped it when my car hit the barrier. I lean back again but look over at the man.

"Thank you," I say to him kindly.

"It's okay, where you headed?"

"Greyton," I tell him, knowing that I won't make Kevin's engagement party.

"I'm headed there myself, is there anyone that I can call?" he asks.

I can tell he's trying to keep me awake, afraid I may pass out or worse, have a concussion.

"My husband," I whisper. "My phone is in the back seat in my bag."

He reaches over to grab my bag and asks if he can open it. I nod slowly closing my eyes, a headache growing.

"Leah Jones?" he gasps.

"Leah Devlin, but how…" I trail off and turn to look at him carefully. He's older now, his tousled hair is now gone and he sports a buzz cut. He doesn't have the beard I'd been used to but it's him. He's in a dark trench coat wearing a tie. It's definitely him, those eyes.

"Leo?" I ask him groggily. What are the chances? I haven't seen him in years.

"Yes, its Leo, wow."

I smile at him weakly.

"My husband, his name is Owen," I say.

"Oh, yes." He looks down at my smartphone and searches my contacts. He puts the phone to his ear and after a few seconds, I hear him updating Owen.

"She's conscious, but still very groggy. The ambulance is on its way. It's no problem at all." He rattles of a number which I assume is his.

"Goodbye." He looks over at me. "He's worried about you, he's on his way, but he'll probably meet us at the hospital."

"Us, you don't have to … I'll be fine," I say.

"It's okay Leah. I would feel better coming along. I'll call Kevin and your family to explain," he says.

"Kevin?" I ask, confused.

"Yes, I am on my way to the engagement party," he says.

I don't know why I'm so surprised, but I can't believe Kevin didn't mention that Leo would be coming.

The sound of sirens alerts us to the arrival of the ambulance and tow truck. My car is plush against the barrier and the tow truck clamps it and moves it away enough so I can get out. My legs are wobbly and I don't dare attempt to stand up. A paramedic rushes over a stretcher which they assist me onto. I'm placed in the back of the ambulance and the paramedics resume with the checking of my vitals.

Leo paces at the door of the ambulance. I can't believe that he is here. It's been years since I saw him. He catches my eye for just a brief moment before he looks away and pulls out his phone.

"We're going to have to take you to the hospital, Mrs. Devlin, just for observations, but it will most likely mean that you will have to stay overnight," the paramedic says to me gently. I nod, feeling helpless.

"Mr. Devlin," he turns back to Leo. I flush at the mistake.

"I'm not Mr. Devlin," Leo responds curtly. "He will be arriving soon. I'll follow you to the hospital all the same."

The paramedic nods and settles into one of the fold up seats beside me. I try to protest, but Leo's already walking away. *He doesn't have to accompany me*, I think to myself, but I know him well enough to know he will, no matter what I say.

LEO

I don't know why I'm here in this hospital hallway waiting to hear how Leah is doing. It's not like she is in a critical condition. It hasn't been in my nature to care for anyone lately, and it frustrates me to admit that I do care about her. I just want to know that she's okay, hand her over to Owen and leave.

Speak of the devil.

Owen rushes in, his hair standing on ends, worry lines etching his forehead. He's taller than I remember and definitely not the bony kid I almost pummeled years ago. I stand up and walk to meet him halfway.

"Hi, Leo?" he asks hurriedly. "Is my wife okay?"

I realize he doesn't recognize me. Have I changed that much? I hate the sound of the word *wife* as it falls so naturally from his lips.

"Yes, she's stable. The doctors are in with her now. I know you. You're the same guy Leah dated in high school, right?" I don't know why I ask that, knowing all of this. He looks at me puzzled.

"Yeah, and you are?"

"Leo Williams. Kevin's friend, I was on my way to the engagement party when I came across the accident."

"Wow, that is such a coincidence, I'm glad you were there, man." He pats my shoulder. The friendly gesture irritates me. The surprise and recognition is written all over his face now.

"Well, since you're here, I'll leave you to it then." I stuff my hands in my pockets and start to leave.

"Thank you, Leo, it means a lot that you accompanied Leah here," he offers.

He is smiling at me and there isn't anything off about our interaction but I can't help but dislike the man. He seems like a nice enough person but there's just something about him that makes me want to punch his face. I should punch his face just for the sake of it. I nod at him instead and make my way to my car.

I leave, not bothering to say goodbye to Leah. I want to get as far away from her as I possibly can. I walk out and the cool air that greets my face is a welcome change from the confines of the hospital, and the smell of antiseptic that hangs thick in the air. I just want to get back on the road, I need to get to Kevin's parents'

house and change out of these clothes that have long since dried and crinkled.

I jump into my SUV, turn up the heat and music and back out of the parking lot, trying and failing to push all thoughts of Leah out of my mind. I don't care that her eyes still look into my soul, that her lips are all that's been on my mind for the last few hours, and that her wild hair is still as beautiful as the last time I saw her. She has a few faint lines that appear next to her eyes when she smiles. It is the only evidence that she has aged at all. I remind myself that I don't care that she still looks incredible, and I continue repeating that mantra as I increase the distance between us.

My GPS thankfully directs me to Kev's parent's house in under an hour, that and my driving. I walk up the familiar pathway and I can't help but feel that this is a homecoming.

I haven't walked this pathway in many years and not much has changed. I've been in touch with the Jones family over the years, always checking in, making sure they're all okay, but I've never visited since -. I don't want to think about the last time I was here and how I felt when I had to turn and walk away from the only woman I have ever loved. I understand why Mr. Jones saw the need to protect Leah from me, and I don't hold it against him. That part of my life is over.

Mrs. Jones still maintains her garden and the sweet smell of well-kempt roses hits me, and I can't help but smile at the comforting aroma. Mr. Jones' old Ford is still parked in front of the garage like it always has been. He never saw the need to use the garage for its actual purpose but converted it into a man cave of sorts, complete with a pool table and mini bar.

I walk up and the door swings open before I knock, Mrs. Jones stands there grinning from ear to ear. I walk up to her and grab her in a tight bear hug. She smells of good food and honey, as she always does.

"It's good to see you, Mrs. J." I set her on her feet and smile down at her.

"Leo Williams, you big oaf, how long has it been?" She smiles. "Where is your hair, Leo?"

"It's been too long," I laugh. "And wasn't it you who told me I should cut off my mop?"

She laughs heartily. It's a familiar sound. She's older, I realize, but she is still as lovely and warm as the day I met her. Mrs. Jones has always been like a mother to me, someone I could look up to growing up. She loves her children and she opened her heart and home to me when I needed it the most. Not just later on in my life, but throughout the time I lived in Greyton.

"Don't catch a chill out there, Leo, get in here," she orders, motioning for me to come inside. The aroma of good food makes my stomach rumble and she pats my belly and tells me to go get a snack.

I really needed to change but there were more pressing matters on hand.

"Mrs. J, can you get Kevin and Mr. J? I have something really important to talk to you about."

"Is everything alright?" she asks hesitantly.

"Yes, don't worry but it's best if I tell you all together." She hurries off and three of them appear after a few minutes.

I greet Mr. Jones and Kevin with a brief embrace and proceed to tell them about Leah's accident and hospitalization. They relax considerably when I assure them she's stable and that Owen is with her. But I can see they're all still very upset and worried.

"Thank you, Leo, we are so grateful that you were there," Mrs. Jones sobs, hugging me tightly.

I later excuse myself to go upstairs to shower and change. Walking into the guestroom that I used as my bedroom all those years ago brings back a flood of memories I don't anticipate. Although the room is completely different than I remember, it still feels the same. The single bed has been replaced with a double bed, the desk drawers have been replaced with a much smaller version. The posters that used to cover the walls have been removed and the wall now houses a large mirror. The dark blue walls are now a light and airy gray to match the bright sheets and covers.

I walk over to the window and push it open, letting the chilly breeze wash over my face and seep into my cotton shirt.

I should have known that being here was a bad idea, but I remind myself that I am doing this for my best friend, my brother. I planned to stay at my guesthouse for the night, but Kevin wouldn't hear of it, neither would his parents. I slip off my shirt and slacks, realizing that there isn't any time for a shower. I am late enough. I pull on a fresh pair of dark jeans and a white button down shirt and run some water on my face before I make my way downstairs.

After a couple of beers, I relax enough to admit that it feels good to be back. It's not a lavish affair with just a few close friends and family. I'm glad that there is no talk of work and my nonexistent love life which is common in my own circle. The conversation steers to Kevin and Tania's upcoming wedding. When asked, I tell them all a bit about my travels and how Liam is doing in Spain. Friends from high school avoid the topic of my shenanigans, probably realizing that is an out of bounds area for me. I've changed, I'd like to think. I smile inwardly as I watch Kevin and Tania together, they do make a wonderful couple and I can see why my friend has decided that it's time to settle down. The food is delicious and I compliment Mrs. J.

Later when everyone leaves, and Tania and Kevin's

parents turn in for the night, Kev and I sit out back with the last of our beers.

"So this is it, huh?" I ask him and he smiles at me lopsidedly.

"This is it, bro." We clink our bottles in unison.

"It's great, that you found the one, Kev," I congratulate him, feeling genuinely happy for my friend. "Some of us are born bachelors."

"Or we choose to be," he corrects me. I laugh at that. He knows me too well. "How's Liam doing really?"

"He is cut from the same cloth indeed." I laugh. "But he's a good kid."

"And Leah?" he asks and I look at him stunned.

"What do you mean bro?" I ask him cocking an eyebrow. "You just spoke to her."

"I mean how it was seeing her again after all these years." He grins. "Look, save me the details, she is my sister, but are you okay?"

"How'd you know about that?" I ask in disbelief.

"There isn't much I don't know, Leo, especially when it comes to my sister and my best friend, plus there isn't a sane reason why you wanted to pummel poor Owen in at the club that night. I figured something was up, that, and my mom mentioned that you two spent a lot of time together before she went off to College. I figured you would tell me about it someday."

I chuckle at the memory of the club and try not to think about the other part.

"It's water under the bridge my friend." I try to keep my tone light. That is one place I don't want to revisit. I down my beer. "Let's call it a night, your father wants to barbeque tomorrow and your mother never lets us sleep in," I say, getting up. We pack up our chairs and toss our bottles in the dustbin.

"I wouldn't have minded you know," Kev grins as we reach the top of the stairs. "You and Leah, back then."

I nod and punch his shoulder. "You need to sleep, bro. You've had way too much to drink."

Lying on my bed that night, I try not to think about the conversation with Kevin or the emptiness I feel in the pit of my stomach. An emptiness I have tried to fill to no avail. I try to fall asleep but knowing sleep has chosen to evade me yet again, I get up, login to my laptop and start on the position paper which is due a month from now. I don't need to think about anything else tonight.

LEAH

I wake up feeling surprisingly better this morning. The doctors even gave me the green light to go home. Owen is sound asleep in the lazy boy next to my bed, his hair stands on end. His phone starts to buzz and he wakes up instantly, reaching to silence it. I smile at him when he looks up at me.

"You're up?" he asks, sleepily reaching for my hand.

"For just a few minutes actually." I smile.

"How are you feeling?" he asks, kneading my knuckles. I like the comfort that simple act brings.

"Much better and so glad I'll be going home today." I beam.

"You scared me there, Leah. When Leo called, I didn't know what to expect." He looks at me sadly. "I'm sorry I wasn't with you. I should have been with you." I feel a sinking in the pit of my stomach at the mention of Leo's name. I brush it off.

"It's okay, O, I'm fine," I try to reassure him. I haven't seen his side to Owen in a long time.

"I just don't know what I would have done if I'd lost you."

"There is no need for that kind of talk now." I wonder if he truly means it.

The nurse comes in and after checking me over, she informs me that the doctor will be in after breakfast to officially release me. I get up, take a quick shower, change into something comfortable and wait for the doctor to arrive. The doctor tells me that I'm home free and it's like music to my ears.

"Do you really have to go to your parents? Shouldn't you just get home and rest?" Owen asks.

"I am fine, Owen, and besides, I missed my brother's engagement party, the least I can do is show up and spend some time with them."

My family called me yesterday after Leo informed them about the accident. They even considered driving out here to see me. I had to plead with them not to cancel the party. I am looking forward to spending time with them.

The hour drive felt agonizingly long especially since Owen and I had drifted back into an awkward silence. My parents were out of the front door before we got out of the car. Mom is in tears as expected and Dad simply hugs me close. It is great to be home. Walking into my family home always brings back comforting memories and the smell of steaks on the grill is amazing. Kevin takes our bags from Owen and tells us to go out back. I step out into the garden and I am surprised to see Leo standing over the grill.

"Leo? Hi," I greet, still a bit stunned to be seeing him after all these years. Despite the fact that he is the one who saved me.

"Hi, Leah," he replies casually, walking over to shake mine and Owen's hands. Electricity courses through me and I pull my hand away. How is that even possible? He doesn't seem to notice, so I ignore it.

"I didn't think you'd still be around. But I'm glad you are, because I didn't get a chance to properly thank you yesterday."

"It's nothing really. Anyone would have done the same thing," he responds nonchalantly.

I want to say that while that may be true, Leo isn't just anyone, but I decide against it.

"Thanks anyway," I smile at him.

He nods and walks back over to the grill. "And I'm still around because your brother bullied me into being his best man," he calls over his shoulder offering me a dimpled grin that almost had me swooning like a teenager. I need to get a hold of myself.

"Steaks are almost done guys," he shouts over to everyone.

I settle in at one of the patio chairs and put my feet

up on the table only to have Mom smack it away.

"You're thirty-four Leah, not ten," She says, and I laugh and curl my feet under me.

Owen is distracted. *It must be work.* I think to myself. He's been under a lot of pressure recently. I tried to convince him to let me take a taxi here so he could head back, but he refused.

I watch Leo from a distance and can't believe how comfortable he still is with my parents, especially with his new lifestyle. I doubt his new crowd would approve of backyard barbeques with middle class commoners. He does look good though, those jeans fit him almost too perfectly and I can tell that he spends a hell of a lot of time at the gym. Tania joins me and takes me out of my reverie. We talk all things wedding and it feels nice to have another female around besides Mom, we'd always been outnumbered with Kevin, Leo, and Dad in the past, and then Owen later on.

Leo serves the steaks, which are cooked to perfection, and we all settle down to eat once Mom and Tania bring out the salads. I love how comfortable Tania is with everyone. Owen always seems a bit awkward with my family, he tries not to be but he can't help it. They can all be a bit much with all the mothering and smothering that goes on.

"So, Owen, you're in civil engineering too?" Leo asks in a tone that makes me wonder if this is some sort of interrogation.

"I am," Owen responds.

"I hear from Kevin that you're pretty busy," Leo continues.

"It gets that way in the industry," Owen answers curtly, obviously uncomfortable making small talk.

"You should tell me about some of your work. I have no interest in the profession itself, but I'm thinking of expanding my investments," Leo proposes.

"Sure, we'll talk later," Owen retorts. I doubt that conversation will ever happen, and I inwardly chuckle at this battle of testosterone going on.

"What about you, Leah, you're a speech therapist right?"

I nod between bites. "Sure am, Leo, how are things on your end? I hear it's a pretty cutthroat business for the high and mighty." I cannot keep the edge out of my voice. I don't know why it bothers me, it just feels like his grilling comes from a *holier than thou* place.

"I guess it pays the bills," he states. I bite my tongue, well almost.

"How's Lucy Smith, have you seen her since you've been in town?" I ask.

"I wouldn't know, Leah, and no, I have not seen her since I arrived. I was too busy grilling your steaks." He smiles at me, but it doesn't reach his eyes, and I know I'm getting to him. We give each other the stare down and I don't care about how it looks to everyone else. Kevin kicks me under the table and I glare at him. My mother's warning glare stops me in my tracks. I am being rude to their guest and they hate that. Never mind the fact that their guest is an arrogant asshole. Owen missed the whole exchange thankfully as he is once again engrossed in his cellphone.

It's strange how a little bit of rain completely changes the way we view things sometimes. One minute, we are enjoying lunch, well most of us are, and the next, the skies open and we are rushing indoors for cover. It is so unexpected and we find ourselves scurrying inside, practically climbing over each other to keep dry. I accidently find myself plastered to Leo's wet chest on the way inside and he moves away so quickly, you'd swear I'd scalded him. I want to brush it off, but I can't help but find his reaction a little offensive.

Owen continues to be restless and I know he wants to leave. I can't really blame him, I would too, if I were him and had just spent an afternoon with Leo and Kevin.

"You okay?" Owens voice startles me.

"Yeah, I'm okay, you?" He's standing in the doorway of my parent's living room, and I can't help but notice yet again how uncomfortable he looks. "I was wondering when you want to head back actually."

Is it really so difficult for him to do this one thing for

me? I never ask him to visit with me anymore because it's usually met with some or the other excuse.

"We just got here, Owen, we can't just up and leave? "I argue, shocked. "We barely finished lunch." I start to pace the room in annoyance.

"Sorry… it's okay, that was inappropriate," he turns to leave without waiting for my response.

I look at his retreating figure and wonder what on earth has gotten into my husband. He is never this edgy or agitated. The Owen I fell in love with used to be fun and up for anything. The stress of his new project must really be getting to him, still, that is no reason to be antisocial.

I stare outside the living room window and watch the rain pelt and slide down the glass. My mother's loveseat still sits just under the window, the blue fabric is worn and the color is not as vibrant as it used to be. I look around me and the room still looks the same, it smells the same too, even after all these years. I walk over to the family wall and notice the new additions. There are pictures of me at college, my wedding day, Kev on holiday, and then my eyes rest on the picture of my eighteenth birthday, which was such a long time ago. I let my fingers trace over the frame and the glass and I let it linger on that familiar face, a face that's aged a bit but is still so incredibly striking. I don't chide myself for thinking it, but smile instead. I hear a clearing of the throat and turn to see Leo entering the room.

"Hi." I flush, feeling self-conscious and wondering if he saw me.

"Hi, Leah." His dark eyes find mine and his forehead creases when he sees the picture.

"It's good to see you, Leo." I know how cliché it may sound to him but I mean it nonetheless.

"Same here, Leah, I'm glad you're okay." He doesn't smile at me but his eyes never leave mine.

"So, you're staying over here too? I thought you'd want to see the house again." I try to sound nonchalant, but I can't stop the heat that creeps up my cheeks when I think about the last time we were there.

He shrugs and walks over to the window and stares outside. "Your parents insisted that I stay here. There is no saying no to them."

"What have you done with the place anyway?" I ask, wanting to make small talk to ease the growing tension in my body around him.

"It's a guesthouse now, Liam's stopover. A local couple runs it for me. I haven't been there in years."

"You really did it all, didn't you?" I say warmly. He doesn't respond, just acknowledges me with a glance over his shoulder.

"It's been a while hasn't it?" There is no need to expand any further.

"Yes, it has been." I walk over to where he stands.

"How are you, really?" he asks, turning to face me, meeting my eyes with his intense gaze.

"I've been good, Leo, I've grown, and life is good." I listen to myself and I wonder who I am kidding sometimes. I say the same line to everyone.

He looks at me as if he wants to say something but thinks better of it.

"You?" I ask.

He considers this. "As you see, Leah. There isn't much else."

I want to expand. I want to know if there's a Mrs. Williams in his life, but I notice he isn't wearing a ring. Still, that doesn't mean anything.

"And Liam?" A small smile appears on his face. It's faint but there. I remember that smile, that old familiarity returning for just a glimpse, it was always there when he talked about Liam. Even back then, he wasn't guarded, he was carefree when he spoke of his little brother.

"He's great." He smiles wider now, his dimples peeking, so much more visible without the beard. I imagine what it would be like to touch his cheek with my palms. I mentally slap myself for thinking it.

"He's travelling a lot so I don't see him as much as I would like to." He sighs. "Anyway, I just wanted to see how you're doing. It's good to see you again."

"Likewise, Leo, Good night."

"Good night." He pauses for just a second at the doorway but rethinks it. He walks away but not before looking back and winking at me.

I laugh, that wink is definitely something I didn't expect.

I lie awake that night, listening to Owen snoring softly beside me, but it's not Owen I'm thinking about. I can't seem to get Leo off my mind. It is probably just the coincidence of him helping me. It isn't unnatural to think about him considering how much I once loved him. I hadn't seen him in years and I couldn't deny that he is still incredibly gorgeous, in that same bad boy kind of way. I found that odd given he is a hot shot lawyer in the city. Whatever it is, I should just forget it and him.

I pull the comforter closer around me, trying to get warm. After a while, I realize it's useless. Sleep has chosen to evade me tonight. I get up, careful not to disturb Owen and tiptoe out of the room making sure the door doesn't creak as I shut it. I walk down the stairs and make my way to the kitchen. I'm surprised to see the light on and Leo sitting at the table tapping away on his laptop.

"Couldn't sleep either, huh?" I ask, making my way to the fridge. I grab a bottle of water and take a seat opposite him.

"Yeah, rough night, so I thought I'd catch up on some work while I'm up." The remoteness is back in his voice, causing me to wonder if that wink actually happened.

"You're different," I consider him. He was different. It wasn't just the way he looked, yes I noticed the specs of grey in his short hair or the crow's feet that only made his face more handsome, no, it is much more than that. He is more guarded, colder, harder and not at all like the guy I had once loved. People misunderstood Leo, they saw the worst in him, but with me, he opened up. He was real. This version of Leo is difficult to relate to. Every time I speak to him it feels like I am in a business meeting.

"Different? How?" He frowns, his signature expression of annoyance.

"It's nothing." I brush him off.

He nods his focus back on his laptop.

"You don't want me to tell you?" I question.

His eyes meet mine and I feel like it's the first time he's actually seeing me since that fateful day on the highway. I feel my chest tighten and my insides clench. His gaze holds me captive. He sighs, breaking the moment.

"You just told me it's nothing, Leah? So why would I ask?"

"Do you have to be such a dick to me?" I hiss. He doesn't answer. "I am trying to make conversation here, Leo."

"I didn't ask you to make conversation with me, Leah."

I feel heaviness in my chest. He really is a cold bastard.

"Well good night, Leo." I get up and turn to leave. He lifts his gaze to meet mine and I feel as if he wants to say something but doesn't, just like earlier in the day.

"I'm sorry. I shouldn't have been so rude."

I want to shove that apology in his face and storm out of this kitchen, but instead I sit back down. "It's okay."

"How are things with your work?" he asks. "It's great that you're doing what you love."

I smile. "It's wonderful, Leo. I love so much of it but I just wish I could do more sometimes."

"Oh and how so?" he asks, and I can tell he is really interested in hearing me out.

"The kids I work with, they're just incredible, but I wish that I could offer them more, maybe a proper occupational therapy center so it's not just speech therapy but holistic treatment."

"So, why don't you do it?"

"It's not that simple, resources and funders are hard to come by for a venture like that. There always seems to be a greater need than kids with learning and speech incapacities."

I can't for the life of me understand why I have just told him my deepest hopes and dreams. I don't know why I feel the need to tell him. I'm at ease with him. I've always been that way with him.

"You know what I think? You're scared, of not actually succeeding with something like that, but you fail to realize how incredible the idea is, you've got to keep trying. Put a business case together and approach companies doing Corporate Social Investment and keep trying until someone caves and gives you the funding." He looks into his laptop bag and pulls out a card, and hands it to me. "Start with this guy, maybe you'll convince him you have something there." He smiles. "Good night, Leah." He closes his laptop and gets up to leave. "Think about what I've said."

"Thank you, Leo, I will," I assure him before he walks away quietly.

I look down at his card and smile, and then switch the lights off and make my way upstairs. I crawl into bed and I sigh loudly, letting go of the breath I'd been holding for what seemed like forever. I turn to my side and let sleep take me, wherever that may be.

LEO

I need to get out of this house, I need to leave, now, there is no use putting it off. I can't be here, in this room and in his house. I need to get home and I need to get away from her. What was I thinking considering investing in her venture as amazing as the idea might be? Leah brings back unwanted memories and unwanted feelings. I don't need this, not now, not ever. But when I exit the guestroom, trailing my bag behind me and I walk past her room and see her sitting on her bed, her head hung low and her shoulders slightly heaving, I can't stop myself from doing what I have taught myself not to do, and that is care and get involved.

"Leah?" Her name escapes my mouth before I can stop it and it sounds sacred. "Are you okay?" I ask hesitantly.

"Yeah, I'm okay, I'm just tired I guess, and the shock of the accident and all that." She wipes her eyes and doesn't look at me. I know that can't be it.

Something in me shifts and I want to reach out and touch her, hold her hand and tell her she can trust me with whatever it is that has put her in such a state, but I can't, or I won't, whichever it is.

"I just want to say goodbye. I'll be on my way shortly."

She looks up but she doesn't meet my gaze.

"Alright, I'll see you around I suppose," she says in a way that doesn't sound like Leah at all.

"Okay," I nod and leave her with her demons. I guess we all have them.

As I take the stairs two at a time, I can't help but feel there's more to her behavior than just the aftermath of an accident, which for all intents and purposes, is minor.

"Leaving already?" Kevin slaps me on the back playfully when I meet him in the foyer. "I knew this small-town thing wouldn't do it for you." He laughs.

I grin and slap him back. His parents join us.

"Not without breakfast he's not," Mrs. J scolds, and I smile at her warmly.

"I wish I could stay, but I really need to get back as soon as possible, I'll have a coffee though and some of those delicious muffins to go," I tease.

"It is great to see you again, son." Mr. Jones pulls me into a hug. "I'll see you at the wedding."

After all these years, I am so glad to have finally gotten close with Garrick Jones again. He is the only father figure I had growing up. It wasn't until after Leah left that we even tried talking about the growing tension between us. It was never that I wasn't good enough for his daughter. He felt she'd been too young to start a serious relationship. By the time we shook hands and made up, it didn't matter anymore. Leah left and she wanted nothing to do with me.

Half an hour later, I'm in my car and on my way home, a bag of muffins and homemade coffee in a takeaway cup. I don't think I have ever been this relieved to be going home. I will miss the Jones' and Kevin, but I'll see him in a few days for the dreaded suit fittings. I turn the music up and try to push away the thoughts of Leah that have started to consume my mind, the sadness in her eyes this morning, which I couldn't begin to understand and above all, take away. It wasn't my job to do that anyway. Doing that once nearly destroyed me and I won't let that happen again.

My chest burns as I run, the rain pelts down on my back and I don't care that I don't have a shirt on, I need to get to her and I need her to understand that what she thought happened didn't. My feet hurt as the gravel scrapes me but I keep running. I can't lose her, I won't. The events of last night come back to me. Lucy Smith needed a place to crash. I couldn't just leave her drunk outside the bar alone. She was beyond crashed. I don't even know how she got to the bar in the first place because her car wasn't even parked out front. Mine was the only one in the lot. I stumbled into my house, dumped her on my couch and I fell into bed, drunk as shit, my head spinning, thoughts of Leah running through my head.

I reach the Jones' front yard and I stop to take a minute to breathe. Her father's car was in the driveway so I know Leah's here already. I knock at the door, hard, she opens it and the way she looks at me makes me want to fall to my knees, so I do.

"Leah," I say her name like a prayer. I'm tired, defeated, and all I want is to hold her close to me and know she will listen to everything I have to say to her.

"Leave, Leo."

Her sadness is palpable and I can't believe I've caused it.

"Please, just come with me, let's go somewhere, just you and me, please, Leah, baby, please." She looks at me and there's only sadness in her gaze.

I want to take it all away. "Let's go away from here, from it all, I'll stay here all night if you want me to," I beg.

"I can't, I can't do that." She's frustrated and looking around anxiously.

"Why not," I plead. "If you love me, come with me." The tears fall from my eyes and onto my cheeks, and I can't stop them. I don't want to. I need her to know it's killing me.

"I love you, I always will, but I can't leave with you, not after

everything, I don't want to hear anything, Leo, I don't need to be a rocket scientist to figure out that you've been messing around, for fuck knows how long."

"Nothing happened with her, Leah, listen to me, and believe me!" I shout. "I was drunk... she was drunk...I couldn't just leave her there."

"So you took her to bed instead?" She looks at me the way they all do, a useless, good for nothing that can't get anything right.

"No!" I shout, trying to reach for her.

"Leave Leo, it's over." She glares at me as if I am an unwanted parasite.

I can't be here, not like this, so I get up and I walk away from her. I stop for just a second. "I would die for you, Leah, give it all up for you. I thought you want the same things I did."

"I don't even know you, Leo. I don't think I ever did. I don't want to see you again," she says with finality.

I walked away from her that day and I swore another woman would never break me or make me feel that helpless or useless again. She didn't listen, she acted like an immature child and I didn't need that in my life then, and I sure as hell don't need that in my life now. Back then, I had to be strong, for me and my brother. I had to be the best man that I could possibly be for Liam. I couldn't let a break up destroy me or deter me from the plans I had for my life. So I didn't look back. I didn't try to call her when she left town. I didn't try to see her. I heard she left for college and that she was happy, and I was happy for her. I heard she graduated with honors, and I celebrated inwardly. I heard she married, and I was content. I always wanted her to be happy. I stopped telling myself that I wasn't good enough. I was simply not the man for her.

I pull into Megan's driveway and I sit there for what seems like forever. I should go in, I should have some fun, and Megan knows how to have fun, but I can't stop myself as I turn the key in the ignition, back out onto the street and make my way home.

I sleep alone that night.

LEAH

It's strange, isn't it, how suddenly you come to see someone you've known most of your life, in a different light? One minute you know all there is to know about them, and the next, you don't. But the scary part is that somehow, deep inside you always know. It's like that awful feeling you get in your gut and in your bones. It's like an infection, which starts in one small part of your body and without treatment, starts spreading, until it's taken over your whole body until it's incurable. I have never been the type of woman to snoop around or question my husband's actions or motives. I have always been happy living a simple life without complications, but there were things that suddenly didn't add up, things I could no longer ignore, no matter how hard I try.

I'd been home alone for a few days. Owen is working on yet another project that required him to travel out of town. He left the morning after we arrived at my parents' house, despite the fact that I didn't have a car with me, despite the fact that we had just arrived there, and despite the fact that I protested and asked him not to. We ended up arguing, as we usually do. Him defending his constant absence, saying it is for us, for our future and me accusing him of not caring enough about me. It ended in him storming off without even saying goodbye to my family. I sat crying for what seemed like hours, wondering where on earth we went wrong. It wasn't supposed to be like this, and no, it wasn't always like this.

Owen and I attended the same college after high school and it seemed inevitable that we'd end up together. There was no question in our second year that we should try the dating thing again. I wasn't keen at first, breaking up and moving on from Leo was not easy, it was unbearably difficult, but Owen persisted, and I caved. I didn't regret it. He was a great guy and a good friend. He made me laugh so much that whatever I was drinking came out of my nose sometimes. He made me smile and did all the things I knew Leo would never have been able to do. He was a good guy and I let him in.

When we graduated, there wasn't a doubt in my mind that he was the man I wanted to spend the rest of my life with. He was kind, caring, considerate and above all, he was honest, the one person I could trust with my life. So when he asked me the big question, my answer was yes. My family was shocked to say the least. My father told me I was rushing into things but I went ahead anyway.

"My head's on straight remember, Dad," I throw his line back to him during one of my visits. Leah does what Leah wants, I guess, and before I knew it we were married. The early years were good, it's what happened after that changed everything, and I need to know where we stand now. This is why I find myself sitting at my kitchen island with Owen's personal laptop open in front of me and a glass of Pinotage in hand. It is rare that his personal laptop is in the house, but fortunately for me, he didn't have a chance to grab it in the hurry to check if I was alright.

I opened up his laptop and started to key in the password I so happened to see over his shoulder as he typed it in one day. "Violet." The screen came to life with a picture of Owen and me at a work function a few years back. It almost caused me to back down. Why would a man with a picture of us as his screensaver have anything to hide? But I couldn't shake that niggling feeling. I took a gulp of wine and started scrolling through his document folders, work stuff, pictures, mostly of us on holiday, some personal folders with his salary slips and CV. There is absolutely nothing out of the ordinary. Owen is meticulous, everything in order.

It is when I am about to close the folder that I spot it, a folder entitled "new folder," like one you would create only to be renamed later. I open it expecting to find nothing but it is password protected. I try the password "violet" again and it's incorrect. I check the details of the file and realize that it was created in 2012. I type in "violet2012" with no result. I give it some thought and try "violet12." I gasp, it's correct. My heart pounds in my chest. The thing about Owen is that he tends to be predictable in certain things.

There are a few "violet" files dating back to 2012. What is violet? Was it a project? I reason, but why all the secrecy? None of his other files are password protected. This is his personal laptop. He works on another one for work. I open the earliest one and it is a hospital bill and quite a pricey one in fact.

"What the fuck?" I snarl. It is for a maternity stay. It couldn't be one of mine. I close the document and start scrolling through the rest of the information. There are scans and bills. What is all this? I didn't know anything about it. There is a blank document too with a Google email login.

I open all the folders which contain bills, property rental accounts, statements for a bank account under Owen Devlin's name which is not our shared account. My head is spinning. I pour myself another glass of wine and log into the email account through his browser and surprisingly, it is already open. There are emails from one person only, Danielle Winston. That name sounds oddly familiar? I open one attachment and almost fall off the bar stool, there are pictures of Owen, holding a little girl. She must be about three or four-years-old and she has his eyes. I have to grip the counter to steady myself.

Hi Owen, thought you'd like to have these. Violet was so happy to see you this weekend. Thank you again.

More pictures…

Owen and the little girl cuddling.

Owen and the little girl at the beach.

Owen and the little girl smiling at the camera and pulling faces.

Owen and the little girl.

Owen and the little girl.

Owen and…

More emails…

Hi Owen, Violet hasn't been well and she keeps asking for you. She misses you. Hope you'll be able to come see her soon.

Hi Owen, we received your Christmas gifts,

hopefully Violet will be able to spend Christmas with you this year. Merry Christmas.

I pour another glass. What I am seeing is obvious, but I need another glass to lessen the blow, maybe a few more. I need the bottle so I start to drink from it, big gulps. When that bottle is done, I get another one, hot tears burning my eyes until I can't see the screen in front of me. I keep scrolling through the pictures. The tears are falling fast down my face, they pool under my chin, they roll between my breasts, and they fall into my glass. The tears fall and they are overwhelming. My heart hurts, my head hurts, and I can't breathe. Why can't I breathe? I need to lie down, and the floor seems a welcoming option. I get off the stool and lie on the porcelain tiles, the same tiles I chose with Owen a few years ago. I lie on it and let the coolness soothe me. I am so tired. I need to close my eyes. I am being dragged back to a place I don't want to go to.

"Owen, we're pregnant." I climbed onto his lap laughing and placed a kiss on his cheek. He smiled at me and nuzzled my neck.

"I'm so happy for us baby," he said in almost a whisper. I know he was thinking about the last time, about losing our first baby bump. I know he doesn't want to hope again for fear of disappointment. I could hear the fear in his voice and see it in his eyes. But I wanted to hope. This was too important to me. I felt

like this was it, that we were being given another chance.

After our first early miscarriage, I never wanted to get pregnant again, all the hopes and dreams, all that should have been and would have been, all lost in the wind. People told us that we'd have more children in the future, that we shouldn't dwell on our loss. We were young, there was so much time they said. But they didn't know how much it hurt. How much it still hurts.

But we were being given another chance. This was it. It had to be. I walked around on a cloud for those twelve weeks, everything was going great and then one night I got up in a pool of blood and in excruciating pain and I knew that our world was being shattered yet again. I didn't know if I would ever recover after that. I found a way to live after that but there was a dark cloud over me and no one could get close enough to let the light in. Owen tried, my friends tried, but the distance between my rational mind and my sanity grew even further, and the distance between Owen and I grew even more. I knew I needed help, so I started therapy and slowly I decided to go back to working again. Working with children helped me, they saved me. But Owen and I never fully recovered. I wondered sometimes if we ever would.

The couple's therapy caused us to fight even more. He was drifting away from me. I could feel it. He spent more time away from home. He didn't speak to me as much. We stopped being close, we stopped having fun, we stopped being us. I kept going to therapy, he never knew about it. I tried to fix myself but sometimes I wondered if I was beyond repair. Those babies were a part of me. They were supposed to be here with me, with us.

Maybe he wasn't happy enough about the babies or about starting a family with me. Maybe, maybe, maybe—all possible scenarios of why we were so estranged drifted through my mind, none of them were real, but they felt real, at least to me. In the beginning, I held onto them as a buoy keeping me afloat in uncertain waters, and I watched as the man I loved slowly slipped through my fingers. I'd suggested we split for a while several times, and every time he refused. He said he couldn't live without me, that I was why he existed. So I stayed and hoped that the next day would be better.

Chapter 15

LEAH

I wake up and my head hurts, I'm freezing but I can't seem to recall why. I open my eyes and everything starts to spin, when it stops, I am staring at my kitchen cupboards. I drag myself off the floor and sit against the island. The nearly empty second bottle of wine is sitting on the floor next to me. I have some of it on the front of my shirt and I've broken a glass.

"No, I will not let this break me," I say to no one.

My insides feel like their constricting the moment the memories of my discovery flood my mind. I find the strength to stand and I know I have to have a shower and decide what to do about all this, but it would be my decision, not Owen's, mine. He had some explaining to do. I deserved that much and thereafter, who the fuck knew.

I dragged myself upstairs a stair at a time. When I enter the bathroom, I keel over the toilet and empty the contents of my stomach. When I'm done retching,

I peel my disgusting clothes off my body, turn the shower on and adjust it to the hottest my skin can stand. I want to scrub it all off my skin, the feeling of betrayal, the unjustness of it all. I want to come out clean and never have to look back and wonder where it all went wrong. I shower until my fingers wrinkle, towel off and make my way to my bedroom. I open Owen's wardrobe and start moving things around, there must be something, there must be, he probably had some hidden hole in the wall with more sordid secrets.

But then I can't take it anymore. I lie on the floor and the wails escape me, I shake and shudder and I feel my heart breaking. Why did it have to be me? Why would he do this to me? He lied, he cheated, and he hurt me. I hate that bastard. I hate him for everything he has that I don't. I wrap my arms around myself. I need to get out of here but I don't know where to go, I don't know what to do. I can't go to my parents, I can't burden them with this. Bea, I need her if she'll have me.

I walk up and ring the buzzer at the up-market apartment building. To think that my best friend lives just half an hour away from me and that we have not seen or spoken to each other in over three years. She was right all along. I just didn't want to hear it. She didn't like the way Owen handled the miscarriages, she didn't like that he didn't support me as much as he should have, and she didn't like the fact that he spent more and more time away from home. But instead of listening, I told her that it is best that we go our separate ways.

The main gate opens and Bea flies toward me and engulfs me in a hug. I can't help but cry. I can't help but enjoy the feeling of contentment that arises within me. She pulls away only to look at me.

"You look like shit." She half cries and half laughs.

"Come on in, honey." I follow her into the beautiful foyer with a stunning high ceiling and a crystal chandelier. We walk toward the lift waving at the security guard at the front desk.

"Bob, this is Leah, she'll be staying with us for a few days."

I look at my friend and love her so much for knowing I need her even without understanding what the problem actually is. I am so grateful that she is with me tonight.

She lives on the fifth floor and there are just five apartments in the building, one per floor. Her apartment or penthouse suite, as I feel is a more fitting description, is modernly furnished in silver and white with splashes of color here and there. It is exquisitely tasteful. It fit Bea so well. The open plan lounge and kitchen area looks out onto the city and has a breathtaking view with floor to ceiling windows. She directs me to the guest bedroom which is to the left of the living room. The décor from the other rooms flow into this one and it looks comfortable and stylish. She places my bags in a wardrobe and comes over to give me another much needed hug.

"I missed you, Lee-bear," she says, holding me tight.

"I missed you too, Bea, so much."

"As much as I want to catch up, I know all you need to do is sleep right now, but I've taken the day off tomorrow so we can talk." She pulls the comforter off the king size bed.

I take off my shoes and am thankful that I am already dressed for bed, I doubt, I could keep my eyes open any longer.

"Bea, thank you." I take her hand in mine.

"Anytime, Leah." She smiles and I know she means it.

I close my eyes and beg for sleep to take me. I don't care where it leads me. I just need to leave reality for a few hours. So when my lids become too heavy to stay open, I am grateful and I slip into dreamlessness.

I wake up to the smell of strong coffee and bacon. I look at my phone and notice that it's ten a.m., but the room is still dark thanks to Bea's fancy shades. I have several missed calls and messages from Owen. He wouldn't be home for two days which is a relief. I don't want to have the conversation we need to have over the phone, but that doesn't mean I need to talk to him at all in the meantime. I get up and use the much too fancy guest bathroom to freshen up. My breath reeks from the red wine from the night before. I brush my teeth until I am certain I wouldn't knock Bea out. I comb my unruly hair and tie it into a ponytail and slipping into a gown. I make my way out of the comforts of this room to face my best friend.

Bea is humming in the kitchen while she prepares breakfast. It is a strange but pleasant sight. When we were younger, she swore she would never pick up a spoon. She swore she wouldn't need to cook, with all the maids she would hire to take care of her every beck and call. I notice that she is wearing yoga clothes and shoes. Her long hair is tied in a tight ponytail, which means she's already out for a run this morning. I love a run as much as anyone, but gosh this weather made it difficult to keep fit.

"Hey." She smiles at me, motioning for me to sit down. She hands me a steaming mug of coffee, milk with one sugar, just the way I like.

"Hey." I smile back, feeling that first sip of coffee as it takes its effect.

"How did you sleep?" she asks.

"Like a baby." I take another sip. "Thank you, Bea." And I don't just mean for the coffee.

She piles two plates with egg whites, sausages, bacon and mushrooms and places one in front of me. I am in heaven. I don't know whether it is the feeling of elation, the amazing smell of coffee, or food that does it, but before I know it I am a shaking mess in my friend's kitchen. She rushes over to me and starts soothing me by rubbing small circles on my back.

"Talk to me, Leah," she urges me gently.

And I do, I tell her about everything I'd learned, all my fears and frustrations and about what I need to do next. She listens and doesn't interrupt. I can see that she is seething but she keeps it under control for me and I love her for that.

"I am so sorry, Leah. I just don't even know how you can face him again without wanting to kill him, heck I want to kill him." She balls her tiny fists.

"I just can't believe he would do something like this and keep it from me all these years, all those times he went away, I just..." I can't even finish my thoughts.

I burst into tears and let my friend soothe me. "Thank you, Bea, for being here for me…" I sniff.

"Always, Leah." We hug and she warms up our breakfast, and we eat it slowly. My appetite isn't great so I just eat enough to keep me going.

The thing about our friendship is that despite the time that's passed, we are able to simply pick up where we left off. It is as if time stood still for a few years and picked up again. We spent the day holed up in her apartment watching everything from romance to horror, she makes lasagna from scratch and it is the best thing I have tasted in a long time. We drink expensive wine and laugh about old times, she manages to take my mind off my troubles for a little while and I love her for that. When it is time to go to bed, I hug her tight and there is no need to say thank you again, the words didn't need to be spoken, she knew.

I hadn't looked at my phone all day and when I picked it up there were over one hundred miss calls from Owen, my mother, and Kevin too. I sigh, it is past eleven p.m. but I know I have to contact my parents. Otherwise, it will cause them unnecessary stress. I decide to take the coward's way out and text them.

I'm okay Mom and Dad, tell Kev too. I'm with a friend, need some time to think. Please don't worry. Love you guys, Lee.

I knew that wouldn't keep them at bay, but I need time to figure out what I plan to do with my life. I see more texts from Owen and the latest one catches my attention.

I'll be home by morning. I love you, Leah. O

I expected that might happen. I am not prepared for

it but there is no use postponing the inevitable. I take comfort in the fact that no one knows where I am or with whom. I will call Kevin in the morning and tell him not to stress, it is a happy time for him and the last thing he needs is family drama.

I don't bother replying to Owen, I don't need to. I am tired of living a lie. It is time to change that.

LEO

I feel restless, I don't know why but I figure it had something to do with the fact that my best friend is so wound up this morning at our suit fitting.

"What's going on man?" I ask when I had about enough.

"It's Leah," he hesitates considering how to say what he needs to. "She's gone AWOL. I mean she sent me a message to say she's doing okay and that she is with a friend and that I shouldn't stress. But how do I not stress, it's not like her man." He shakes his head.

"What about Owen, doesn't he know where she is?" I enquire.

"That's the thing, he doesn't, she hasn't even contacted him, and so I am guessing he has something to do with this disappearing act of hers."

"I'm sure everything is okay, Kev, like you said, she isn't like this, and she probably just needs space. Maybe they had a fight or something? She's a grown woman bro, give her some time, she'll talk to you when she's ready."

"You're probably right, Leo," he lets out a breath he has probably been holding all morning.

Well, I hope I am right. I don't know why it bothers me as much as it does. I have been having sleepless nights since I saw Leah again, but I know I need to get her off my mind.

Sitting in my office, later that day, I realize that I am not being productive. I take my suit jacket off the hanger and rub my hands across my face. I need a distraction so I tell my PA I'm leaving and before I know it, I am taking a drive over to Megan's house.

"Well, hello stranger," she purrs in that sexy sultry way as she opens the door to let me in.

"Megan," I greet her without smiling.

She shakes her head. She walks over to the living room and takes a seat on one of her plush couches, motioning for me to do the same on the one across from her.

"Where have you been?"

"Around," I answer, not wanting any more chit chat.

"So did you miss me?" she asks, getting up and sauntering over to where I sit.

"Less talk, Meg," I grab her around her waist bringing her to me.

She is a beautiful woman, tiresome but beautiful. She has curves in all the right places and beautiful light brown hair and eyes that make her look fierce. We'd known each other for years, each of us happy with the friends with benefits arrangement.

She straddles me, unbuttoning my shirt. I respond to her as I always do, with an intense fire and overwhelming need. I feel her mouth on mine but then unwanted thoughts start entering my mind, thoughts of a woman with unruly brown curls and eyes that looked at you with interest, as if she listened to every word you say. A woman with her heart and soul, lips that you wanted to kiss all day and every day.

I looked at Megan and as much as I want her and this, I can't. I pulled her toward me and hold her close.

"I'm sorry. I'm just not myself today," I say, kissing her hair.

She looks taken aback, she didn't expect the sincerity in my voice and neither did I.

"Who is she?" An amused expression dances on her face as she hops off me and sits beside me.

"No one," I say, angry that she would jump to conclusions. She smiles knowingly.

"Let's have some dinner and wine." She laughs.

"That, I can do."

There were days like today when I wondered what

it would be like if I had taken the time to get to know Megan, or any of the many women I have been with over the years. Women are complicated and from a young age I realized that relationships were just not for me, until Leah. Leah made me want more, she made me want to be a better man and then she went and threw it all in my face. She made me realize that everybody would always come to the same conclusion about me, no matter how much they claimed to love me. I was a fool for giving my heart to her and that is one mistake, I vowed never to make again.

All those years ago, all I asked her for was a chance to explain, for her to hear me out, and she could not do that. I was just a complication in her life and she deserved better, and I agreed because she did deserve better. I grew up hearing I was not good enough and she confirmed that, that was true.

LEAH

He's sitting on one of the stools in the kitchen when I get home, hunched over the counter. His shirt is crinkled and his hair is standing on ends. This isn't the Owen I am used to, but who is he anyway? He turns around and he's not alarmed to see me standing there. He doesn't make a move toward me. He just sits there, his eyes red like he'd been crying all night. I doubt he slept at all. He looks like shit and I wonder if it is a ploy for sympathy. I'm all out of sympathy. This will be quick and painless and then he will leave, because he cannot stay here another second more than I want him to.

I'm cold inside, I feel like all the feelings have been drained from me. I don't smile. I don't feel anything toward him.

This is the man I married, the man who swore to have and to hold me, from that day forward, for better, for worse, for richer, for poorer, in sickness and health, until death do us part. He said those vows and slipped a ring on my finger and promised me forever, that I would be the only one, always forever.

He lied. He lied. He lied.

I don't hate him. *Hate* doesn't adequately fit how I feel. I could gut him now and not feel a thing. I walk around the island and sit across from him, my back straight, head held high. He looks at me and looks smaller than I remember, like he's shrunk somehow. His handsome face looks old and worn and I want to laugh at him, so I do. My laughter booms across the walls and he looks shaken, not knowing how to react. He rubs his face across his hands. He knows he should start talking or walking. The latter won't be a good option for him.

"I'm sorry," he whispers. I continue laughing. It's an ugly sound. I hate the way it grates in my throat. I'm manic, I look at him and he rubs his hands across his face. I like the tiredness in his eyes, I like the way his hair looks ugly and dirty.

"I need to start at the beginning, Leah, and I need you to know that this isn't an excuse, there is none that can justify what I have done. There is nothing I can ever say to make this better, but I know I need to say this to you. You don't have to understand and you don't have to forgive me, but please just listen."

I look at him and stop laughing, but I say nothing.

"After losing the second baby, you went into your own world, I just couldn't reach you. You refused to go for help no matter how much I tried to push you into it."

I did go for help, you bastard, you just didn't know it.

"You would look at me and not see me. You were going through life around like the walking dead. Nobody could reach you. You retreated to a place where I couldn't reach you anymore." I lost a child. We lost a child. That is understandable. You acted like nothing happened. I look at the pathetic excuse for a human being in front of me and I have to keep myself from vomiting as the bile rises inside my throat.

"I was away for a week on one of my projects when I met her again, Dani, it only happened twice, I didn't mean for it to happen and afterwards I wasn't in touch with her. I knew her when we were in high school and we fooled around back then. It was nothing serious back then. It wasn't anything serious when it happened either. I felt like shit when it happened and I didn't want anything to do with her after that. I made sure that she corresponded with someone else on the project from then on. A few months later, she contacted me to tell me she was pregnant and that I was the father. I didn't believe her at first so we had a paternity test done and Violet is without a doubt mine.

I couldn't leave her, Leah. I couldn't not support my child, but I couldn't lose you either. So, Dani and I kept in touch, but only because of Violet. Dani is engaged now. I left in such a hurry the other weekend because she and her fiancé are moving to New Zealand with Violet once they get married. I wanted to try to reason with them."

You have a child with someone who is not me.

The tears stream down my cheeks gently and I feel them join at the base of my chin and fall down my neck. I wipe my eyes and walk over to the fridge and grab a still water and sit back down. I still haven't said a word to him.

"I'm sorry, Leah, I'm sorry, I'll do anything to make this better." He tries to reach out to me but he fails to realize that it'll never be better.

"Leave!" I shout. He flinches and looks like a fool. "Leave, and never come back." I am surprisingly calm.

He looks as if he doesn't understand what I am saying to him.

"If I could help it, I wouldn't speak to you, but I suppose I have a lot that I need to say, Owen."

I pick up my water and take a long swig, and then throw the half full bottle across, missing his head by inches. It bounces off the wall and lands on the floor.

"These last few days have been hell and right now I feel numb. Things were never perfect between us over the years, but we were good together, at least I thought so. We took vows, Owen, vows, and I kept them, I kept them and you didn't. I am hurting so much right now and I know I can't and won't be able to get pass this. This isn't something I even want to think about working through."

"Leah please, please just listen to me, we can work this out, if only you'll let me try." He stands up to make his way over to me. I put my hands up to halt him.

"It isn't something that's negotiable. I know I will never feel differently about any of this because it's all wrong, Owen. You cheated, period, you lied, you made a fool of me, and you have a child with someone else and a life outside of all this." I motion between us.

"I'm sorry, Leah, please, just let me try to make this right." He pleads.

"You had a good few opportunities to do that over the years and you didn't, you could have told me when it happened or even a year or two later but you thought you could keep this from me. How fucking long did you think you could hide this from me, Owen? Forever?" I shout. "It's been four fucking years for god's sake!" I shout at him, getting up and making my way to the front door. I open it and stand there for a while waiting for him to join me.

"Get the fuck out, now!" I scream, my hands shaking.

I remember the day we bought this house, I remembered him carrying me over the threshold, me giggling uncontrollably. I remember the nights we spent making love in each room, eating on the empty living room floor. I remember our first couch, our dining room table with the warped leg, I remembered the times he hung paintings and stood back to make sure they were hung right.

But I also remember the sadness and coldness when he'd leave me alone for days and weeks on end. Time he spent with his whore and his child, a child we would never have, playing happy family mocking me.

"Leave, Owen, you can come back for your stuff tomorrow when I'm at work, get someone to move you the fuck out of here because if you don't, then I fucking will, "I hiss coldly.

He walks toward me and I shudder as he leans down and places a kiss on my forehead.

"I'll make this right Leah, even if it takes me a lifetime." That is a fucking long time to wait for something that is never going to happen.

"You're more insane than I give you credit for, Owen." I shut the door in his face.

I can shut the door behind him but I can't shut out the pain inside me. I scream at the closed door, banging at it with my fists until they hurt. My heart feels like it is being squeezed, like all the life will leave me at any second. My head hurts like no oxygen is reaching it. I sink to the ground and I cry. I cry for everything we should have been, I cry for the babies who never lived, I cry for the life we should have had, I cry and I beg for the pain to end. All I want is for the pain to end.

Being cheated on and betrayed by the one you love is something no one should feel. When you decide to be with someone, you let them into your heart and soul and you trust that they will take care of it, of you. He lied to me and there is no moving on from this, well not together anyway. I go to the kitchen and get a bottle of red wine, no glass necessary. I start taking large swigs from the bottle and make my way up to our room, *my* room, I remind myself. The room we spent years in together, sharing a bed, fucking, sharing hopes and dreams.

I start pulling out every last suitcase we own and proceed to drag his color coordinated wardrobe into them. His stuffy suits that hold no appeal to me now. Which one did she stroke and remove? When the suitcases were full, I zip them up and get black dustbin bags from downstairs, along with another bottle of wine. I then proceed to dump everything in the dustbin bags. I take down all the pictures of us I can find and box them. He could have them if he wants. I pack his toothbrush and toiletries, and after three hours I felt like I've packed Owen away completely.

But he is still everywhere. He's chasing me down the hallway and whacking my naked ass with a towel. He's all around me, so I go downstairs to the bar and pour myself some whiskey. I then pour myself some more. Tomorrow I will figure out what to do, today I would let alcohol do that for me. I open my handbag and take out a small business card. I want to forget so I dial the number on it.

LEO

It's one a.m. and my cellphone is ringing. I don't recognize the number and decide it must be a wrong number. But the caller persists another four times before I answer.

"Leo Williams," I growl, feeling irritated, as I should be. No one calls me at this time.

"Leo Williams, that sounds so serious." She attempts the worst possible impersonation of my voice. I don't need to guess who it is. The voice that haunts my dreams has just awakened me from one.

"Leah." I sigh.

"Yes, it's Leeeaaah," she stretches her name out and giggles uncontrollably. I hear something falling over and crashing in the background. Why would she be calling me so late?

"Are you okay, Leah?" I ask, frustrated.

"I just have one question for you, Mr. Williams," she slurs.

"Okay." I can tell she's drunk and drunk calling is never a good idea.

"Is there something wrong with me?"

I yawn. "What the fuck is this, some sort of trick question? No, Leah, nothing's wrong with you, where are you?"

"Home, I'm at home. If nothing is wrong with me, why would he hurt me, why did you hurt me?" She starts to cry, and as much as I don't want to feel anything, I do.

"Who hurt you, Leah? Can I come over?" I ask.

"No, you didn't answer me, Leo," she insists.

"I will when I see you, Leah. Where's home?"

She rattles off an address which isn't too far away.

"I'll be there soon, baby." I cut the call, pull on my sweatpants and t-shirt, heading out at one-fifteen in the morning to make sure my ex-girlfriend is okay. But my biggest concern is why the fuck I called her baby?

I pull up to the nice suburb. The address she gives me is a nice house on a cul-de-sac, pretty, a double story place with an open lawn in the front, with some sort of small fountain. There are a few lights on downstairs so I make my way to the front door and knock. She doesn't answer the first few times, so I call her number back.

"Leah, it's Leo, I'm outside your house, open the door," I grunt.

"Noo…" She slurs. "You can't be here, why are you here?"

"Open the fucking door, Leah, or I'll break it down."

A few seconds' later she unclicks several locks and lets me in grinning.

"Are you alright?" I demand, frustrated, raising my eyebrows at her.

"I am. I was just out of wine," she whines, nuzzling up to me. "Don't be so grumpy, Mr. Cranky-Ass."

"I think you've had enough wine for one night, how about bed?" I suggest.

"No, Leo, I want some wine." She pouts with her hands on her hips. She is the cutest fucking drunk in pink pajamas I have ever seen.

I look at her and I know there is no arguing. If I don't get her wine, she'll go try and get it herself in that state.

"I know just the place," I smile even though I try not to.

"Okay, whoopee!" She strolls outside barefoot.

I shake my head, lock the door behind me and catch her before she falls flat on her face on the front lawn. I set her into the passenger seat of my car.

"This is a nice car, Leo, it's warm and cozy." She leans her head against the headrest looking over at me like I am her favorite person in the world. I turn up the heat and make my way to the best wine joint in town, my own cellar. I told her that she would ruin me all those years ago and in this close proximity, nothing seems to have changed.

As we pull to a stop, she opens her eyes and beams at me.

"You live here?" she asks in wonder. I nod.

"It's huge, humungous huge, enormous." And even though I don't want to smile again, I do.

"Come on. Let's get you some wine then," I jump out and let her out.

She follows me in and she seems to be taking everything in. She wanders into the living room, it's dark but the moonlight casts a dim light that surrounds her like a halo. She truly is a beautiful woman, effortlessly so, pink pajamas and all. I turn the lights on in the foyer and living room and ask her to get comfortable. She walks around, touching my furniture and paintings, in awe of her surroundings.

I don't get a lot of visitors, especially ladies. I haven't exclusively dated anyone long enough to bring them home and yet, here she is, Leah, the one I have fought for years to forget, getting comfortable on my couch cross-legged and giggling like a teenager.

I leave her and walk to the kitchen and open the door leading down to the cellars. I am not here often and if it wasn't for Jana the place would be covered in spider webs. I turn on the dim lights and decide to choose a Merlot. She looks like the red kind of woman. I'm about to turn around and head up the stairs when I feel her arms snake around my middle. The feeling is foreign, yet familiar. For a moment, I forget to breathe as I feel her head resting against my back.

"Thank you, Leo."

I turn around to face her and it breaks my heart to see tears forming in her pretty brown eyes. I take her hand in mine and lead her back to the living room. Dim light, closed spaces and a beautiful woman aren't a safe combination, especially when all I want to do is kiss her tears away and make everything okay again.

I grab a glass on the way and we take a seat on opposite ends of my two-seat couch. I pour her a glass and hand it to her.

"You're not drinking?" I shake my head and let her gather her thoughts.

She tucks her wild hair behind her ears and since I last saw her, tonight she looks more like my Leah than ever. She's older yes, a thin line appears when she crinkles her eyes in concentration, but she's still the loveliest thing I have ever set my eyes on. She is beautiful in every way, in every sense, inside and out. I remind myself that Leah is a married woman.

She sets her glass down and seems to struggle with finding her words.

"You don't have to talk about it now, Leah," I

offer.

"I want to, Leo," she says thoughtfully and I realize that she actually needs to talk about it.

"Owen and I got married just out of college. He was a great person and it just made sense since we'd had a thing back in high school, well until you of course, "she blushes. "We loved each other as best we could and we made each other happy most of the time. But as with most married couples, the trials seem to be the great test. We both wanted children but sadly we lost two babies, both in my first trimester. The doctors say I have irregularities in my uterus which didn't allow my babies to survive. I've been on treatment ever since but we sort of gave up trying after a while.

It was too hard and hurt us both too much. I guess we accepted the fact that I will not be able to carry a baby to full term. But accepting it and living it are two different things. I ended up in a dark place for a very long time, battling anxiety and depression. Owen used to be supportive at first, but then he started spending more time away and that should have been a warning sign for me." She takes a minute and breathes. I get up and turn on the gas fireplace which heats up the place nicely.

"Anyway, to cut a really long story short, I just found out that my husband has been having an affair and has a secret lovechild with his work colleague." She stands up. She's slightly unsteady and she starts to pace the room. "How could I not have known all this?"

"I'm sorry, Leah, truly I am." I don't have the words. She feels defeated, humiliated and betrayed and I understood that. I just don't understand what I can do to help her. Why would she reach out to me of all people?

"I gave him years of my life, Leo, for nothing," she continues. I stand up and make my way to stand behind her.

"I thought he was the right person for me. I thought I was moving on from loving you to someone else. But right now, here I am cheated on, living a lie all these years, and I don't know what is right anymore. I just know one thing…" She trails off turning to me. She places her small hand over my chest and my heart starts to race. For a moment, I think I'm going to pass out.

"I gave him all I had. He was everything to me for a long time, and I want to change that now. I want to change that with you, no strings attached, no relationships, and no complications." The words leave her mouth fast and her eyes are ablaze and full of determination as they meet mine. I haven't been this close to her in such a long time. If I wanted to I could take it just the way she said, no strings attached. But I need to reason with her.

"Leah, I know you're hurting and you think that this

is the best thing to do." I motion between us. "But I can't let you do this. I don't want to be yet another regret you have."

"Don't refuse me, Leo, not tonight," she pleads.

She starts to lift my t-shirt slowly, her eyes never leaving mine. Her hands roam across my bare chest and down to my abs. She wraps them around me, digging her nails into my back. She traces her way back to my stomach and starts drawing an invisible line with her fingers downward, until she reaches the hem of my sweatpants. She allows her fingers to hook and roam around the band, never taking her eyes off me. She bites her bottom lip and smiles at me seductively, her eyes aflame. I know I shouldn't do this, but my primal instincts betray me. She awakens something animalistic in me and I find myself lifting her off her feet and carrying her up to my bedroom. I place her on my mattress and watch as she clumsily tries to remove her pajamas.

"Let me." My voice is hoarse. I slip her top over her head in one smooth movement, and her breath hitches as my eyes roam over her beautifully exposed breasts in a white lace bra. I slide her pants down her legs gently. She is so incredibly breathtaking. I revel in the fact that she is here with me, in my house and in my bed. I could do this. I could give her what she needs and forget about it. I've done it before, many times, she's no different.

I kiss her lips and she moans into my mouth. The familiar scent and taste of her drives me insane, and my initially gentle kisses become more intense. I want to claim her. I want to own her, if only in this moment. It's been years since I'd held her like this or kissed her lips. I trail kisses down her neck and onto the swell of her breasts while my hands worked her nipples gently through her bra.

Her body molds into mine and she holds onto my neck, pulling me closer to her, her hips grinding into my hardness. I start to unbuckle her bra but stop, out of breath. As much as I want to do this now, there is no denying that this is Leah Jones and there was a time, not that long ago, when she meant more to me than just this one-night stand. She is still more to me than that. Kissing her gently, I look into her eyes. "Not tonight, baby girl, not like this, you're drunk, you're hurting and I can't add to that. Just let me hold you," I whisper, letting my head fall to her chest, hearing her rapid heartbeats slow down. She wraps her arms around my neck, holding me closer to her chest.

She is broken and this isn't how she is going to piece herself together again.

I look up at her and see the tears falling from her eyes and I kiss away each one before taking her into my arms, her back to my chest. I hold her tight and when her breathing evens, I allow exhaustion and sleep to take me.

I know it will be difficult to let her go again.

LEAH

I wake up with a splitting headache. I am surprisingly warm and comfortable. The arms wrapped around me hold me tight and make me feel secure. I could stay in this cocoon forever. I look at them and gasp, they're unfamiliar. Where am I? I turn around. *Leo*? The events of last night are a bit vague. I look down at myself and am horrified that I am in nothing but my most revealing underwear. I hop out of the bed not sure what the fuck I've done or what even happened.

"Hey, hey."

"Don't hey me," I shriek.

"Whoa there, nothing happened, come back here." He yawns, motioning for me to join him as if it is the most natural thing in the world.

I'm too embarrassed to face him so I grab the nearest piece of clothing and slip it noticing later that it's his t-shirt.

"Leah, come on, nothing's happened, you drank

too much and you needed to crash," he says lazily. He doesn't seem like he has a fucking care in the world.

"So what, you took advantage of me, how could you?" I shout at him angrily.

"Trust me, it wasn't me making the moves, Leah," he tells me cockily.

"You bastard." I gather my scattered clothing items, feeling utterly annoyed that it is just a fluffy pair of my pinkest pajamas. I am so frustrated that I am obviously in his house and I've slept in his bed all night. I flush at the thought of what could have happened between us.

"*You* called *me* last night Leah, let's not get into name calling, shall we?" He throws the covers off himself and standing up to reveal his well chiseled chest and gray sweatpants that fit him just perfectly. I wish he wasn't as gorgeous as he is in that moment.

"Like what you see?" He laughs making his way to what I assume is his bathroom.

"I hate you, Leo Williams!" I shout.

"Heard that a million times, baby," he shouts, while taking a morning piss quite loudly might I add.

"I'll be leaving thank you." I leave the room taking the last remnants of my dignity with me. How could I let this happen?

I take the long staircase downstairs and can't help but notice how beautiful this house is. It truly is luxurious and so unlike the Leo I once knew. I make my way to the foyer where I hope I'll find my bag and keys but I look around and there is nothing. I check the living room and kitchen and decide to just wait for him to come downstairs and tell me where my stuff is. I sigh and take a seat at his kitchen island, my hands covering my face.

"I drove you here," he answers the question I didn't ask. "Coffee?" He walks over to the granite counter and slips a capsule into the machine. He places a cup in its place holder and in a few seconds a delicious steaming cup of coffee sits in front of me. He passes me the sugar. Just one and doesn't bother passing me milk. He remembers.

"How could you drive me here?" I frown, taking a sip of the heavenly concoction in front of me.

"Well, you called me and I came over to your house, you wanted more wine and this was the only joint open." He motions around him. "After a while you started making moves on me and one thing led to another. I said it wasn't the right time, it got late, we fell asleep and now we're here having this conversation, like I am the bad guy." He turns around and switches the coffee machine on again.

"How is it that I am always the bad guy?" he asks, more to himself, his voice laced with amusement I don't feel.

I sigh and decide he has no real reason to lie to me.

I need to pull myself together. My brother's wedding is in a week and he doesn't need a basket case of a sister spoiling everything for him.

"I'm sorry, Leo, and thank you, I didn't mean to offend you," I say awkwardly.

"None taken, babe." He flashes his dimples at me and making me wonder what it would be like to stick my fingers in them again.

No rebound has ever proved to be a good thing, I remind myself. I have been through hell and back the last few days and the last thing I need to do is complicate my already complicated life by getting involved with someone else. With Leo.

He sips on his delicious smelling cup of coffee.

"What's with the buzz cut?" I ask more to make conversation.

"I don't know, new me I guess." He grins. I detect a hint of something else behind those words, but decide that it isn't my business.

"Would you mind calling me a cab since I don't have my car here?" I ask

"I can one up on that, pretty lady, I'll take you home. Want to shower?" he offers, winking.

"I…err."

"I didn't mean together, Leah, but if that's what you have on the mind, I suppose your wish is my command." He bows dramatically.

I laugh at him then, grateful that for the first time in hours, I feel a little bit lighter and like myself.

I know I have a long road ahead but I can do this.

One step at a time.

LEO

I want to hurt him the way he hurt her. I want to find him and smash his face in but I know that won't do Leah any good. When I dropped her off earlier, everything in me wanted to stay, to protect her. But I knew that would complicate things even further. He is coming over to collect his things and I don't want to be in the way of that.

I don't understand why I am allowing myself to get so deeply involved. I shouldn't get involved because it has nothing to do with me. But, I can't help but hate the sad look in her eyes. She deserves better, better than Owen, better than me even. She deserves someone who would make her happy and smile all the time. She deserves a hero, a savior. Not that she can't do all of that on her own, she is obviously strong, brave, and highly intelligent, but a woman like her deserves someone in her corner.

I promised her that I won't say anything to Kevin.

It isn't my story to tell. She does not want to tell him anything until after the wedding.

I make my way to the place I dread the most, the hospital. This is a routine checkup I'd arranged for myself with my physician, Dr. Peters.

"Mr. Williams, hi." I am greeted by a burly man in a baseball cap who is dressed like a doctor, but who looks more like a lumberjack.

"Yes, and you are?"

"I'm Scott. Dr. Peters couldn't be in today so he asked me to fill in. How are you feeling today, Mr. Williams?" he asks.

"On top of the world, Doc, call me Leo," I respond as he goes about the routine checks, drawing blood and writing up x-rays. I feel strong but according to my specialist, Dr. Evans, I am not out of the woods as yet.

"Well it looks all good so far, we'll get the blood work back and then we'll know for sure."

"I know for sure Doc," I sigh.

I dress quickly, wanting nothing more than to be out of this place.

"I'm off for the day. You want to grab a beer?" I am slightly surprised by his request but he has a likeable face so I nod.

"Why the hell not?"

We agree to meet at a bar not far from the hospital. A small hole in the wall place I assume the guy frequents. It is called The Olive Bar. We order some beers from the bar, non-alcoholic for me, and grab a table by the window.

"Nice place," I motion around me. The décor is rustic. It is a really nice set up. The bar is small but not cramped. There are tables lining the window and a few at the back. The bar looks like something out of an eighties movie, all dark mahogany. The lighting is dim but it didn't give the place a dingy vibe. There is a grand piano on one side and I wonder whether Leah would like to come with me to a place like this. She used to play the piano in school, I never heard her but Kevin said she had talent.

"It is." He clinks his beer mug to mine. A waitress comes up to our table and smiles at us warmly.

"What will it be, boss?" She looks at Scott.

"Wait, this is your place?" I laugh.

"Heck yeah." He beams.

I shake my head. This guy is odd. Physician by day, bar owner by night.

"We'll have the chicken wings, Kira. You high flyers eat wings, right?"

I laugh at that. "It is great that you have this." I look at the paradox before me in awe.

"Can't just have a day job right, you've got to do what you love too."

At that moment, I realize I like Scott, I like his hon-esty and his zeal for life. I can see us being friend's.

We spend the afternoon drinking beers and talking like old friends. Besides Kevin, I didn't have many male friends. My professional circle is big but my social circle isn't. But sometimes it's nice to talk to someone you're not exactly hiding anything from. Scott's biological parents died at an early age and he moved from foster home to foster home, until his family adopted him, set him straight, and got him through medical school. He has a younger sister in London.

His adoptive mother passed away with cancer, the silent killer of men. He opened the Olive bar in honor of her. She always encouraged him to live his dreams. Scott is surprisingly still single and not interested in relationships. He is a self-proclaimed free man with not a care in the world. I leave the bar liking Scott a whole lot. He is a good guy to be around.

LEAH

It is Kevin and Tania's rehearsal dinner tonight, and thankfully, Owen has sense enough not to show up. He knows better. After collecting his things, he attempted to call and stop by several times, but I told him where to get off. My lawyer already drafted the divorce papers and served it to him, although he has not signed it yet, it is all over for me. I need to move on with my life and I need to be happy. There was too much of time wasted on a man who did not value our vows or me. I did not need him complicating my life any more than he already has. As difficult as it is to fall asleep alone at night, I know someday I will rise above this, stronger. Like a Phoenix, I will rise from the ashes of my pain. I have not told my family about the separation yet. I want my brother's wedding to go off as uneventfully as possible.

I feel strong in my gray silk evening gown that fits and flows perfectly down my curves. My hair is loose and wild with just a silver leaf pin hooking up one side away from my face. The hotel ballroom is beautifully decorated. The chandelier cast a glimmer across the room and reflects off the immaculate silverware. It is the kind of scene one could lose themselves in and I did, for a few moments. I let myself forget that I am alone, that my husband had betrayed me, and that I often feel broken. If you can savor just one moment at a time, that is survival. I am surviving.

"Penny for your thoughts." I look up to see Leo staring down at me. I hadn't even seen or heard him approaching. He looked gorgeous in his tux.

"They're not interesting enough to make me rich."

He laughs, and there are those dimples again. My heart skips a beat just looking at him.

"Leo, I don't think I actually thanked you enough for the other night, you didn't have to be there for me, but you were and I'm grateful," I say meaning it.

He simply nods and takes a sip of his orange juice.

"You don't drink?" I motion to his glass.

"I kind of get out of control when I do," he smiles. "How are you though?"

"I don't know how I am right now, Leo, honestly, but in time I will."

"I know." He traces my cheeks with his knuckles. My skin burns under his touch and he moves his hand away and clears his throat when he realizes what he is doing. I feel the absence of his touch immediately. "I'd better be the best man," he backs away.

"You already are," I whisper to myself, and I gave him a small wave, and chastise myself for feeling and thinking like a hormonal teenager.

"And what was that all about?" Bea hisses in my ear. "Leo?"

"What about Leo?" I play dumb.

"The whole sexual tension, touch your cheek, back away nervously thing you two had going on?" she asks too loudly.

"Long story, Bea, long drunk story," I whisper.

"We have time, spill," she demands, pulling me aside.

I spent the next few minutes regaling my drunk calling, almost sleeping with Leo fiasco. By the time I finish, I do not think I have seen such a shocked expression on my best friends face before.

"Whoa, that's something, so you guys going to hook up or what?" she asks.

"Gosh no, Bea, that was a one-time thing, a drunken mistake I don't intend to make again, besides, that isn't what I need right now."

"It is exactly what you need. A hot guy all over you is the ultimate heartbreak cure."

"Bea, it's not that simple."

"Then make it simple, Leah. But right now, I'm not going to lecture you, I am far too interested in that surfer guy over there."

"That's my cousin, Bea, he's half your age, don't spoil him for the rest of the world." I laugh as she saunters over to my cousin Jason.

"Is everything alright, honey, I notice Owen isn't here?" The moment I'd been dreading had arrived.

"He's working tonight, Mom, he really regrets not being here but duty calls," I try to conjure up my most cheerful voice. She looks at me worriedly.

"You know you can talk to me if you need to, Lee-bear?" she offers.

"I know, Mom, let me go see if Tania needs some help." I hug her briefly and head away from her with my cheeks flushed.

I sit across from Leo at dinner, even though he is part of the wedding party, he is somehow placed there, and I suspect that Bea had something to do with the swapping of name cards.

Kevin and Tania look radiant and happy at the head of the table, barely able to keep their eyes and hands off each other. My parents and Tania's parents sit across from each other and it seems they are all getting along well. I like the chatter. It keeps my mind off my own troubles.

My father, as the father of the groom and host, gives

the welcome toast and talks about the joining of the two families. His words wrap around me and I feel safe, here with my friends and family so close. My mother says a few words after him and has us all in tears, her being no exception. *This is a happy time*, I remind myself, taking a sip of my fourth glass of champagne. I feel Leo's hands on mine, and look up to meet his gaze.

"Slow down," he mouths, and I could have sworn he asked me if we could go somewhere else.

He didn't let go, but started tracing light circles on the inside of my wrists which completely distracts me. The room seems to shift a little. Everything starts to become a bit of a haze, and the next thing I know, he's asking me to dance with him, leading me by the hand to the dance floor.

He wraps his arms around my waist and places my hands on his chest. His movements are slow, precise. I try to flow with him but I'm dizzy. The music is something soft and sensual.

"Look at me," he whispers, and I do. I look into his eyes and everything seems to fade away as we sway to the song I recognize.

He starts to sing to me…

Someday, when I'm awfully low
When the world is cold
I will feel a glow just thinking of you

And the way you look tonight…

The intensity of his gaze and the strength of this hold, cause me to sway even more than I should. I place my head on his chest and listen to the rhythmic sound of his heartbeat, his voice, and breathe against my hair.

It seems like we've been on that dance floor forever, I want to stay there forever, but the music ends and my brother is whisking me away from Leo for his own dance. I look over Kevin's shoulder and Leo just stands there, his hands in his pockets, his eyes never leaving mine and I can't breathe at the intensity of the way he looks at me and the fact that I still have feelings for him, even after all this time.

LEO

I don't know why I did it, but I asked her to dance. The feel of her body melting against mine is amazing and I feel like I will lose myself again, lose myself to her, fall under her spell, never to be revived again. She is everything I need to take another breath, pure oxygen. But I cannot do this. She'd been through enough in her life and I don't want to complicate her life any further. So, when Kevin asks to cut in, I am relieved, but as I watch her walk away with Kevin, I wonder. I wonder whether I will ever be brave enough to let her go again.

I watch them dance and laugh and I like the fact that they are still close. She needs that now more than ever. What that bastard did to her is unforgivable. The music changes and she makes her way back to where I am standing. She leans in close enough that I can almost taste her.

"We should leave now," she whispers breathlessly. I

know she's feeling it too. The pull.

"We should?" I ask. I look into her eyes.

"Yes." She nods, not taking her eyes off mine. She takes my hand and pulls me to the exit. My mind is saying that this isn't a good idea, but my body and heart are saying something else.

"Okay, Leah, let's just say bye to everyone."

"No," she says powerfully.

I open the door for her when the valet brings my car around and she gets in silently. She doesn't say a word as I drive her to my house, and I wonder if she's having second thoughts. She looks beautiful tonight, it's like she gets more beautiful every time I set eyes on her. The years have definitely been kind to her. She is a sight to behold. Her long hair cascades down her slender back, and I imagine what it will be like to slip my hands around her and feel her smooth skin again. But this is her decision. She has to be in control of whatever happens tonight.

She looks outside the window and I turn on some soft music. She smiles, so I know she approves. She lets her head rest on the headrest and I wonder where she goes in that moment. Is she thinking of me? Is she thinking of her stresses and troubles, or simply being at peace and at one with herself. She places her hand on my thigh, and I have my answer.

I pull up at my front door, not bothering to take my

car around. Someone would do it eventually. I run around to open her door and she places her hand in mine.

"Ever the gentleman, aren't you, Williams?" she says, leaning up against me and nipping my bottom lip between her teeth.

The air is electric between us, and the moment I close the door, I back her up against it and my lips collide with hers. My tongue finds its way into her mouth to dance with hers. She presses herself to me, wrapping her arms around my neck, and I can feel myself hardening against her. She tastes amazing and she feels amazing. No matter what happens I would have this night, I would have her.

I unzip her dress and let it fall to the ground, pooling like silver around her perfect legs. I run my fingers through her hair and she leans into me. Our lips meet again, the need, the want, and the desire burning as our tongues twirl. She climbs into my arms and wraps her slender legs around my waist, holding onto my neck and balancing against me. It takes everything in me not to take her right there. I carry her upstairs, not breaking eye contact, and place her on my bed. I remember the last time she was in my bed, her now sexy black lace underwear a contrast to the pink pajamas. I smile at that and start to undress for her slowly, first my jacket and shirt and then my pants, knowing she likes the show as she bites her bottom lip. She squeals for me to get into the bed.

Towering over her, I let her hands roam my body first. I let the feel of her burn into my flesh and my senses. I start trailing kisses down her neck all the way between her breasts. I come up to kiss each swell and squeeze them together, making her moan. She slips her hands into my underwear, removing them, so she can feel my hardness. Her touch is absorbing. I continue my kisses across her belly and finally make my way between her thighs. She moans and pushes herself into me. She shakes her head.

"Now," she moans.

I stop and carry her onto me so that she's straddling me, letting her know that she is in charge. Unhooking her bra, she lets her breasts free.

I am speechless at the sight of her and place my hands on each one, squeezing gently. She moans and throws her head back. She moves her underwear aside, and with one swift movement, she is on me. I feel her tighten around me. Her pace is slow but calculated, and we met each other with every movement. I hold onto her hips and rock her gently. She leans toward me and looks into my eyes.

"I think I still love you, Leo," she moans, and that is enough to push me over the edge.

LEAH

We can't get enough of each other. Being with Leo again is like nothing I'd experienced before. He is gentle, warm, yet intense. We spend so much time lost in each other that I realize that I am falling for him, hard and fast. I don't know what is happening to me. Yes, we have a history. Yes, we loved each other once, but what I am feeling now didn't make any sense. We have breakfast in bed and make love again, getting the food all over the bed. We shower and I hold onto him, not wanting to let go. The wedding is in a few hours and Leo has best man duties. He brought my dress to me and I dress hurriedly.

Driving to my house, I hold his hand, loving the security of his grip. I am still so broken, but somehow, he makes me feel whole. He shuts off the engine, bends over to kiss my cheek, and then jumps out and opens my door. As we walk to my front door, I lean into him not caring if the neighbors see us and think I am messing round. Stopping at my door, I turned around to face him, and he backs me up against the wall for one last kiss before hurrying back to his car. "Later, baby," he shouts.

"Later!" I shout back, feeling like a hormonal blushing teenager. Maybe I am rushing into this. Maybe it's just lust. Maybe I miss Owen and I'm lonely. Whatever it is, it's happening fast and I have no way to control it.

The chapel is beautiful. It is set in the middle of lush green gardens surrounded by trees. The smell of freshly cut lawn and flowers surround me as I walk through the front doors. The sun shines brightly and there is an electric vibe of excitement in the air. Family and friends are arriving, and as I stand outside the chapel I feel more at peace than I have in a long time. I open the doors and the wedding planner is doing her final walk through, her nervous energy is palpable. The chapel is not large or overpowering but it wasn't small either. It is decorated with white and peach roses, which layer at the front of the chapel, and smaller bouquets are attached to every pew, with white silk ribbons hanging from them. The chapel itself is old and looks like something from another century. It is beautiful and I can't wait for Tania and Kevin to see everything.

A red carpet runs from outside of the chapel to the

pulpit. Although I am not religious at all, my parents and brother are, and I imagine a stiff Minister giving a sermon of thou shalt nots. I take a seat in the front row as I'd already been to see Tania, she is radiant but I can't wait for Kevin to see her.

The pews start filling up and I am not surprised that Owen shows up or that he sits next to me. He greets me and I ignore him. He busies himself on his cell-phone and I don't really bother with him anymore. My parents show up and hug and kiss us both. I cringe when he slips a hand around me as some kind of show of solidarity.

My parents sit next to us and I swear that I am changing all the shades of red in anger and embarrassment. Soon Kevin and Leo appear from a side door. They both look dashing in their matching tuxedos. I smile at Kevin and he blows me a kiss. I love my brother and I am so happy for him. Leo arches an eyebrow at Owens close proximity, and winks at me, causing Owen to look at me in confusion. I flush and put my head down and wait for the entrance of the bride.

And when she does, it is as if the world stands still. When the pianist plays Michael Buble's *You and I* there isn't a dry eye in the room. Tania looks like a princess in her white silk and lace gown as she walks down the aisle toward the man she loves. I can't keep my eyes off her and I can feel Leo's gaze on me. I meet it and it feels as if the whole world disappears. It's just him and me, and I burn at the core with need. I break the spell first and concentrate on the ceremony. I actually like the Minister's speech after his sermon about marriage being about commitment and fidelity, and how one should not harden the heart of the one they love by committing unspeakable acts. I take the time to throw a glance Owen's way, and I don't think I've ever seen him blush as much as he did in those forty-five minutes.

The ceremony ends beautifully and as I make my way into the reception hall while the remaining family photographs were being taken, I am cornered by Owen who wants to talk.

"I don't want to speak to you, Owen. We have nothing to say to each other," I growl.

"I said I am sorry, Leah."

"And I said I don't give a fuck," I hiss.

"Is it because of him, is it because you're fucking him now?" he asks, and I assume he's talking about Leo.

"What I do and don't do is none of your business, Owen. I suggest you get that straight," I say making to leave.

"You will not leave me, Leah, I made a mistake, but we can make this all better again," he barks, grasping my arms.

"Let go of me!" I try to struggle from his grasp.

"Leah, we can work this out," he insists.

"I think she told you to let her go, asshole," Leo growls from behind me, making me sigh in relief.

"Stay out of this, Leo, she's my wife," Owen says proudly.

"I am not your wife," I argue, spitting the words in his face

"Oh, yes you are," He is still tugging at me, causing my arm to ache.

Before I know what is happening, Owen is on the floor bleeding from the nose.

"I thought I told you to leave her the fuck alone," Leo snarls, earning us a few glances from the growing crowd of onlookers. "You are not worth the ground she walks on," Leo spits.

Owen stumbles to his feet, his nose bleeding, and his clothing ruffled. "This isn't over!" he snarls, and then he leaves.

I breathe a sigh of relief and let Leo wrap his arms around me protectively. I let him comfort and soothe me.

"Leah?" My dad's voice shakes me. "What's going on here?"

"Are you alright, baby?" Mom asks frantically.

"I'll explain," Leo whispers into my hair.

"No, I have to do this." I kiss him on the cheek and thank him for being there when I needed him.

We find a quiet spot and I finally let my parents in on everything I have kept from them for too long. My mother crumbles in tears and my father ready to erupt.

"Why didn't you tell us all of this sooner?" he asks, his fists balling so hard I can see the white of his knuckles.

"I didn't want to worry or upset you. For the most part, I thought he was just away for work," I say in my defense.

"Leah, we could've been there for you, we could have supported you!" Dad shouts. "You didn't even tell us about the babies. How can you do that Leah?" He gets up and makes to leave.

"Dad."

"Not now, Leah, not now, it's your brother's wedding. Well talk about this later," he dismisses me.

Somehow, I know we wouldn't talk about it anytime soon. I'd hurt my dad by keeping them in the dark about the hardest and darkest times in my life. I didn't want them to worry. I didn't want them to see me as a failure. I nodded and let him leave. My mother wraps her arms around me.

"We love you, Leah, Dad is just upset because he wants to be there for you in those dark times," she plants a kiss on my forehead. I wonder whether she can read my mind sometimes. "Just give him time." She sobs. "I'm so sorry, baby, for everything, we're here now and we won't let him bother you."

I hug her tightly and rebuke myself inwardly for not letting them in sooner. They are my parents and heaven knows I need the support now.

"Can we go party now, Mom?" I ask with a sniffle.

"We sure can," she wipes away a stray tear.

Walking into the ballroom, which is arranged to perfection, is like walking into a fairytale. The peach and white from the chapel carries through with the addition of several magnificent centerpieces and crystal angel lights dangling from the ceiling. I make my way over to Kevin and Tania and hug them both a little longer than necessary, wishing them all the love and happiness in the world.

The truth is that life with Owen wasn't perfect, but it was good when it was good and I would hold on to that. I wouldn't tell people not to marry because of what had happened to me because in truth, I'd experienced some incredible highs with him. On the other hand, I am also a realist and I know that when one partner crosses the line the way Owen did, the other doesn't always have to try to make things work. Sometimes you have to live each moment and see where it takes you, to find who you are or who you need to be.

I look over at Leo and smile. Somehow, I know who I am meant to be, when I am around that man.

LEO

Looking at her across the room with Kevin and Tania, she truly is breathtaking. Her emerald green dress hugs her curves in just the right way, and her hair is swept up, exposing her elegant neck. I want to ask her to dance, to wrap my arms around her and sway to the music, but after everything that's happened with Owen and her parents. I don't know whether it's appropriate. But even more, I don't know that I should do this. Last night with Leah was sensational. I'd never experienced anything like it before, but I know that I can't commit to her, or anyone for that matter. That isn't in the cards for me, and yet, when I look at her, I want to hope, I want to dream, I want to believe in things that will never be possible.

Life isn't fair and I detest that. Why can't I have this? Why can't she have me? I will give her the world, I know that. Make all her dreams come true in a heartbeat. I don't care if she can't have children, I would be happy enough just to have her. We could be content together. We could make each other happy. I need her in my life and she needs me. I am falling for her and I know I shouldn't, not just for me, but for her. This will end up hurting her more than it would ever hurt me. I have to get it together. She looks over at me, and I smile at her despite myself, and my body makes its way toward her even though my mind tells me it is a bad idea.

"Penny for your thoughts." She smiles, causing me to smile back.

"You, baby, can have them all." I give her a swirl.

"You know my brother wants a word, right?" she laughs.

"He is my best friend. He can have as many as he fancies."

"Smart ass." She giggles.

The wedding dance song, Ed Sheeran's *Thinking out Loud,* starts and we watch the newlyweds dancing. I wrap my arms around her waist and gently sway with her, planting kisses on her ear and neck.

"I want to make it through this wedding dance, Leo Williams," she whispers, and I smile into her neck.

"Dance with me."

"Shouldn't you be dancing with someone from the wedding party?" She laughs.

"I only want to dance with you," I whisper.

I can hear her breath hitch as she leans into me.

"Okay," she whispers.

I spin her around and take her hand and lead her onto the dance floor with a few other couples. As we dance to the music I look into her eyes and I hate myself for allowing her to fall for me, because I can see it as she looks up and smiles, as her eyes dilate, as her breathing quickens, and as her hands wrap around me, and finally as her head falls against my chest.

Don't say the words, Leah, or I'll have to say them back.

We dance until the song ends, then we dance until Kevin asks to cut in. I dance with Tania and she grins at me.

"What are you doing, Leo Williams?" she asks sweetly.

I'd grown quite fond of the little redhead since I'd met her.

"Dancing with you, sister-in-law." I smile my most charming smile and spin her around the dance floor eliciting a shriek of delight.

"I don't mean with me you fool." She rolls her eyes.

"Just being there for her when she needs me, Tan," I give her another swirl.

"Take care of her heart, Leo, from what I hear, and it isn't much, she isn't in a good place right now."

I think about that for a second and know she means well.

"I will, Tan, I promise." I don't know what comes out of my mouth these days. I meant to say we're just friends, I meant to do that but I couldn't because looking across the room I know I want so much more, so much more that I can have or give.

Despite the voices inside telling me otherwise, I take Leah home that night and make love to her in front of the fireplace, setting aside all my reservations and reasons for why this shouldn't be happening.

"So what, you're not going to tell her?" Scott says, raising an eyebrow. "She did say she thinks she loves you right?"

I sigh long and hard. "If I do, she'll just feel sorry for me and pity me, I don't want that, I want to just be me, Scott," I growl. I know I sound harsh but he knows I don't mean to.

We are sitting at the Olive bar and he is drinking more than he should as usual. He is on his third beer and I am on that non-alcoholic crap. I need something stronger but I doubt my liver can handle what I have in mind. Scott and I have been meeting here weekly and every time I like him a little more and feel like I know him somehow. He calls it like it is but he doesn't judge.

"Man, it's obvious you love her too, let her in, and no more advice after this, I'm playing."

I laugh at my friend as he makes his way over to the piano. He plays badly, so badly I wonder why he does it. I wonder at times why he is a Physician and not just a bar owning philanthropist but we'd had that conversation before. He'd split his heart in two but overall, he just wants to help people, soothe them and bring them comfort. He says that doing both the things he loves makes him, him.

I wish there were more Scott's in the world to go around.

Leaving the bar that night, I ask my driver to drop me off at Megan's house. I had not seen her since we had dinner together two weeks ago. It was clear that out friends with benefits, relationship was over and I just needed to make that official. She understood, as I knew she would. We hugged and I chose to walk home instead of calling my driver. It is a long walk and my chest hurts but I need to clear my head. Scott is right, I do love Leah, I never stopped loving her, but I would not be able to give her the life she deserves. She deserves so much more than what I have to offer her. The cold night air makes me wrap my coat closer around me. I need to create some distance between us. She needs to have some options. I just wish I knew how to make my heart stop feeling like it is being ripped out of my chest.

LEAH

"Twice, what the fuck, Leah, and you didn't tell me?"

"Bea," I hiss at my friend, "we're at lunch remember, a public place." My face flushes.

"And you said you love him?" Her eyes form large circles which make her look like one of those *Bratz* dolls.

"I said I *think* I love him, there's a difference, and it was in the moment, Bea," I say, rubbing my hands through my hair in frustration.

"Well, you should have told me. I mean I missed the wedding because I still can't get over the fact that Kevin married Tania instead of me." Her sarcasm knew no bounds.

"Bea, you never liked my brother, you just wanted someone to go down on you and he didn't want to take advantage of his little sister's best friend…" I shake my head. "That, and you were working," I correct.

"Oh… the travesty..." she feigns hurt.

“Bea, be serious.” I roll my eyes at her.

“Leah, you’ve just got out of a shit relationship where your husband basically hung you out to dry, the rain has come, revel in it.” She smirks.

“You would say that.” I laugh.

“Seriously though, if it’s good, it’s good, enjoy it while it lasts. Stop committing your heart and soul and just live, you deserve that more than anyone and he’s hot as f-”

“Don’t you even,” I giggle, loving my best friend more than anything. “He’s invited me to dinner tonight at his place. It’s been two weeks since the wedding and I haven’t seen him, I mean we talk all the time but it’s not the same.”

“Then go ask for third’s, girl,” she laughs and I playfully smack her arm.

I have no idea what to wear. I have nothing to wear, a whole closet full of absolutely nothing.

After pulling myself together, I choose a simple black cocktail dress I’ve never worn before and a pair of red stiletto heels Bea got me a few years ago.

I instinctively choose red lingerie, flushing.

Leo arrives at exactly six-thirty p.m. to pick me up despite my insistence on driving there.

I open the door and I’m taken aback by how hand-

some he looks in his charcoal slacks, white dress shirt and black blazer.

"You look stunning, Leah." He kisses me on my cheek and hands me a bouquet of red roses, which I place in a vase immediately.

On the way to his house, he plays some slow jazz and holds my hand in his lap. When we arrive, I'm surprised to see Kev's car in the driveway.

"They're back?" I ask excitedly. I haven't seen them since the wedding.

"They are," he turns off the car.

"I'm sorry I haven't been in touch enough for the last few weeks, I needed some time to think and time to process all this, us."

"It's okay, Leo, it's been a crazy time for the both of us. "I wring my hands in my lap.

"Leah, I just… you mean a lot to me. I need you to know that."

"*Dido*, Leo." I smile.

He walks me up the path, his hand on the small of my back and opens the front door. Tania bounds up to me in seconds.

"I missed you guys." I hold onto them both.

"We missed you too, Leah," Kevin responds.

Dinner is incredible, made by Jana. We sit chatting and drinking the rest of the night catching up on their honeymoon.

I ask to be excused to use the bathroom and close the door behind me, needing a second to breathe.

A few minutes later, Leo comes in and locks the door behind him. My breath hitches when I see the voracious look in his eyes as he walks toward me. Before I know it, he's carrying me onto the basin. He lifts my dress lifts, revealing my red lace underwear.

His hands move everywhere, setting my body on fire and his gaze never leaves me.

He slides me gently forward, tilting my ass and slipping my underwear off.

"Not here, Leo, they're in the other room," I moan.

"They're dancing," he almost growls. "I've missed you." He unzips his pants and lets it fall to the floor.

Suddenly, he's filling me, not gently this time. He rocks into me hard, his need obvious. I hold onto him and try to mute my moans in his shoulder. He feels exquisite.

"You feel so good," he whispers into my neck.

"Leo," I hiss his name as I fall apart. He joins me seconds later, thrashing into me.

He holds me close, and then kisses me gently and sets me on my feet, which are unsteady now.

"I don't know what this is, Leah, but I can't get enough of you. I need you." His voice is desperate.

"I need you too, Leo." I kiss his forehead.

We straighten up and join the others in the living room, and thankfully Kev and Tania are still lost in each other.

We wave goodbye to Kev and Tania later that night.

"Stay," he says, wrapping his arms around my waist.

"There's no place I'd rather be," I say, leaning into him.

Over the years, there were parts of me that died. I was like a fire which isn't nourished, I found myself fading to dust. There were parts of me that I didn't think I would ever get back. Maybe I should have given more of me to Owen, but then I remind myself that even from the start, all he tried to quench my fire, instead of fanning it to brilliance. Leo ignited that flame within me, and I feel more alive than I have in a really long time.

Chapter 26

LEAH

It's been a week. A week since he's called me. I'd even been to his house and no one seems to be around. I called his office and his assistant informed me that he is away. He could have let me know he would be away. He could have told me he is busy. This felt like déjà vu, the times spent away from Owen. I can't believe I've been this stupid. I can't believe I did this to myself again. I couldn't call Bea about it, she would just tell me to get over it and find someone else to party with. But it isn't like that with Leo. I know he feels it too, the connection, something that has always been there between us.

The knock at my front door startles me. I look at the time and it's past nine. Who could that be? I open the door and there he stands. The most beautiful man I ever laid my eyes on, the same, except he looked tired, pale, worn out, and his hair is all shaved off. I slap him hard and then slam the door in his face.

"I'm sorry, Leah." He sounds defeated.

I open the door a little. Tears form in my eyes.

"Why didn't you tell me where you were, Leo?" I whisper. "You could have texted me, anything." I hate how vulnerable I sound.

"I know and I'm sorry. A friend of mine is really sick and I had to take off and make sure he is okay. I didn't have my charger with me so when I got there. I just prayed you'd understand when I saw you again. I'm really sorry. Please just trust me."

"How is he?"

"Who?" he asks.

"Your friend, Leo?"

"Not great, but he's surviving."

"Good, you want some dinner?" I open the door to let him in.

"I'd love some." He holds me close when he's inside. He doesn't let go for a while.

There is something about the way he's acted, how defeated he looks that makes me realize that there is more to this, more to what he's telling me. But I don't want to pry. It isn't my place to pry. His appetite isn't great. He basically moved his food around the plate a few times.

"Would you like to watch a movie?" I suggest.

"I'd love to, your choice." He smiles.

I choose *The Notebook*, one of my all-time favorites, and we cuddle together on my couch. Half an hour into the movie, he is asleep on my stomach snoring gently. I turn the volume lower and settle into the couch and close my eyes. I run my hands over his smooth head, missing the prickle of the buzz cut but thinking how handsome he still is. I don't want to wake him, lying here like this is perfect.

I must have dozed off because when I get up, Leo is carrying me upstairs. He sets me down on the bed and kisses me on my forehead.

"Stay," I whisper dozily.

He gets into bed behind me, pulling me close to him. "I think I love you too, Leah," he says sleepily.

I smile as I drift off to sleep again, content.

LEO

"I'm not one to dish out lectures, Leo, you have Evans for that, but I think *'I love you'* translates to '*It's about fucking time I told you that I'm sick*,'" Scott states seriously, an eyebrow rises in what must be dissatisfaction.

"I know, I know, I just didn't expect to fall this hard for her."

"And now that you have, you need to let her in, Leo."

"Have you talked to Kevin or your brother?"

"No, they would just worry, Scott." I rub my hands across my face in frustration.

"Take it from me, they want to know, they need to know, it will in a way give them more time," he says thoughtfully.

"When my mother was diagnosed, it was the hardest thing on my family but I can't imagine not knowing and having her suddenly leave us, without warning. It brought us closer together as a family. It gave my father more support. My sister, Willow, the traveler, moved back home and got to spend six months with my mother before she died. Just think about it, Leo, it's all I'm saying," he cautions.

I know he is right, I know that they all deserve to know, and now that I'd let Leah into my life again, she of all people should know. I am angry, so angry that I don't have enough time.

"None of us knows how much time we have, Leo." He cuts into my thoughts, almost reading my mind. "But we make each day count. The truth is that you need them," he continues.

"Thanks, Scott, you're a pretty deep guy when you want to be," I laugh.

"Don't tell the chicks, man." He scowls.

"How come there isn't anyone special in your life, Scott? You seem like a genuinely good guy with that whole boy next door vibe. Chicks dig that?"

"I just don't have the time for that, man, I have enough on my plate, then I look at the challenges relationships bring you guys and I decide I'm better off." He smiles and gives me a slap on my shoulder. I don't miss the hint of sadness in his words which he tried so hard to hide or the darkening of his mood. I wonder what his story is.

"I need to drink."

"One non-alcoholic beer coming right up." He motions for the waitress.

After my conversation with Scott, I know I've got to tell her. It will be difficult but I have to. I arrive at her house around seven and everything is dark. I hope she's home before I lose my nerve, I should have called, I realize, because she could be out. I decide to call her cell and there's no answer. I can't decide whether to wait or come back later. The latter seems the more reasonable option but I haven't known myself to be reasonable, not around her.

I get into my car and lean my head on the headrest. If I'm going to have something real with Leah, I have to let her into my life. I have to let Liam and Dale in too. There is no way that I can leave the most important people in my life in the dark. I decide to call Liam but his phone goes straight to voicemail. *This isn't my day, I guess.* I leave a message for him to call me, the minute he stops having fun wherever he is. I smile at the thought of my brother travelling the world. I am proud of the young man he has become, and I wish so much that I could be around to share in his life. I guess that wasn't meant for me.

I put on some music and I must have dozed off because before I know it, I open my eyes and my clock displays one a.m. I looked at Leah's house which is still in darkness and my phone. No missed calls. No messages. Something doesn't feel right, and then I hear it, the faintest sound coming from inside her house and I am on my feet in no time.

LEAH

"Don't move," he whispers.

I am standing at the kitchen sink washing my hands after preparing dinner when I am startled by Owen.

"What do you want here? You're not supposed to even be here," I warn him.

"This is my house too, Leah, remember?" he counters.

I notice that he looks slightly unsteady, like he's been drinking.

"I have company coming over anytime now and I think it's best that you leave." I gulp.

"You mean your new boyfriend, Leah?" he slurs.

"Leave, Owen, before I say something you may not like." I angrily throw a dish towel at him.

"I am not leaving here until you tell me you're giving me another chance," he slurs.

"I am not going to say that, Owen. This. Is. It. We are through and you better get used to that," I say more confidently than I feel.

"You can't do that to me." He stands swaying back and forth unsteadily.

"You did this, Owen, you did, not me!" I shout.

He comes toward me and I back away from him toward the back door. A drunken-soon-to-be-ex is never a good idea.

I turn to make a run for it, knowing the back door will be open, and that's when I feel it, a pressure against the back of my head. I feel dizzy and find myself falling to the ground, unable to control it. Just at that moment, every goes black.

"Leo—" I whisper.

I wake up and I'm very groggy, as if I've been in a deep sleep for a really long time. My head hurts. I try to feel the back of my head, and realize my hands are tied to the foot bars of the mounted stools in the kitchen, and then I remember Owen.

I look around and don't see Owen anywhere. There is a broken wine bottle on the floor, its contents spilt all over the floor and the cupboards, and on me too.

I realize that it's what he used to hit my head.

"Owen!" I shout my voice shaky.

"Tsk, tsk, tsk, Leah, Leah, Leah, baby, look what you make me do." He looks at me sympathetically.

"You won't get away with this Owen, someone will come. I gasp, the air taken from my lungs.

"No one is coming, Leah, we're all alone here, at least for a little while," he sneers.

"What the fuck do you want?" I ask him, struggling against my restraints.

"You, Leah, I want you. We are so good together, you and me, we are great in fact."

"Until you decided to fuck someone else, Owen!" I shout. I hated the crudeness but I hated the man before me more.

"Technicalities, sweetheart," he mocks, taking a sip of what I imagine must be his expensive bourbon. "But I agree that we need to get down to business." He is almost too calm, sitting down on the floor next to me and stroking my hair. It is then that I notice he has on leather gloves.

I've known this man practically my whole life, we grew up together, married for love, not convenience or necessity. But at this moment, I doubt for the first time that I know him at all or even that I will survive this, but why is he doing this?

"I've got myself into a bit of a fix, Leah. Living two lives didn't do too well to my finances. You know how it is? Having a child to support? Oops, sorry, you don't know anything about that, do you?"

I can tell he's lost his mind, but still it hurts. It hurts a lot. It feels like a knife is being twisted into my heart and soul.

"What's happened to you, Owen?" I ask, a stray tear rolling down my cheek.

"I realize that I need collateral. Without you in the picture, I can have that, Leah. When we were together, I wouldn't have imagined doing this, but I dipped into our joint savings too much and it's practically depleted."

"You didn't..." I whisper.

All the money I'd been saving to put as security for the Centre, it couldn't be gone.

"I needed the money, Leah, and you had it," he sputters.

I cry then, thrashing against the restraints, banging on the kitchen island.

He slaps me hard and I can feel the sting even after he removes his hand.

I scream and he put his hand over my mouth and starts to bang my head against the tiled floor.

"You are making this so difficult, Leah, so difficult. It's a pity an intruder broke into the house, robbed you of our valuables, and left you for dead." He sighs. "An unfortunate incident, so sporadic in this neighborhood," he adds. "We're not divorced, Leah, and I have made every attempt to reconcile, besides, and I am out of the city this weekend, business trip." He scoffs.

It hurts, everything hurts. I want to sleep, close my eyes and make the pain go away. I try to pull on my restraints again but that just earns me a kick in the shoulder.

"Let's not make this harder, Leah, let's be reasonable about this," he regards me with mock compassion.

I realize that he's completely insane and someone like that is more dangerous to me than anything.

"Owen, please…" I beg. Hating how defenseless I feel, hating the way my voice sounds, and the way my heart feels.

He lifts my stone grinder from the counter.

"I always hated this thing, but now I suppose it comes to good use," he toys with the grinder.

I know it weighs a lot. I didn't have to know how much.

I watch as he lifts it high in the air, his eyes cruel and derisive. I watch as he swings and then comes a crack and he is falling on top of me, the grinder rolling to the side.

LEO

I see him through the kitchen window and I know that I have to be stealthy. I go around the house again and try the front door, locked. I'd never been one for picking locks, even in my younger rebellious days, so I need to think fast. I go around the side and as if the universe is in my favor, a window is open, one that does not have bars and is large and low enough that I can climb in. I remove my shoes and throw them in the grass, climbing through the open window slowly, hopefully unheard. I hear them talking, her voice low, scared. His voice mocking, mercilessly, and it makes me angry, but I know I have to keep my head on.

I don't have my gun on me. I own one but never carry it. I regret that tonight. I could have blown the fuckers head off here and now. I look around for a weapon and my eyes land on the bar. I creep to it, hearing only the sound of my breathing. I pick up an open bottle of bourbon, I hate the smell, the taste, everything about it, but it is just the thing I need for what I have to do. I put the cap back on. It is about half a meter between where I am and the door leading to the kitchen. He has some classical music playing which scrapes on my nerves. What the fuck is wrong with this asshole?

I make my way to the door but stay in the shadows. He is standing at the kitchen island and I assume over her. She keeps whimpering and saying things that are inaudible. And that's when I see it in his hands, a stone grinder, a heavy thing. He looks at it like a prized possession. I don't have time to think, just to act. I close the space between us in seconds and bash him over the head with the bourbon bottle. He falls in slow motion, landing right on top of her small frame. I pull the chunk of filth off of her, she is completely out of it, I check her pulse, she is fine, and I'd made it.

I hear a shuffle and realize he is getting to his feet. My fist connects with his jaw before he could get up any further, and he howls. I straddle him and start punching his face repeatedly until all I see before me is a bloody mess. I hear the sirens and I can't stop, I hear the crash of the front door and the footsteps approaching, but my anger won't let me.

"Back away, sir," I hear the commanding voices of what I assume to be the police.

The next thing I know I'm being dragged off an unconscious Owen. *I shouldn't have called them*, I think. I need to finish him for the pain he caused her. I look over at her and there is a policewoman kneeling over her checking her vitals, and I cry. I cry a gut wrenching cry because I don't know what I would do if I'd lost her.

The paramedics arrive and move her onto a stretcher. They set him on one too. They ask me if I am the caller and whether I would make it down to the station to answer some questions. I shake my head. I need to go with Leah. I need to know that she is okay. The policewoman tells me to come by as soon as I am comfortable that Leah's condition is stable. I agree.

I get into my car and bang my fists into the steering wheel. I sat out here all night long, and I should have been inside there doing something. Why didn't I know something was off? I follow the ambulance cursing myself for not being there when she needed me, for not protecting her from that monster.

LEAH

I wake up to the beeping of machines in the hospital. The events of the night come flooding back and I shake with fear. Strong arms surround me and I shudder.

"Don't hurt me," I whimper.

"It's me, babe, it's me," Leo soothes. "He's not going to hurt you. No-one is."

He wraps his arms around me and I let myself dissolve into him. I cry then, for the pain in my head and body, but mostly for the pain in my heart and soul.

"Shh, baby, you're okay now, I promise," he soothes.

He takes a seat at my bedside to give me space but his eyes and hands never leave mine.

"I don't remember getting here." I sob.

"I got there in time, the police and paramedics arrived just after."

"And him?" I ask, I see his eyes heat up with unspoken words of anger.

"Recovering, but he'll be locked away for a long time once he's awake and stable," he spits.

I nod, wiping a stray tear. My head really hurts. I lift my hand to touch the lump which has formed where the bottle hit me.

"There are no fractures, just deep bruising and swollenness. You'll be your old self in a few days," he mumbles, more to himself than me.

"Thank you, Leo, for arriving when you did, you have a habit of saving my life," I smile.

He doesn't smile back, instead he looks at me intently.

"I have to go down to the station now and give a statement. Your parents are here. Kevin will be here as soon as he can." He leans down to plant a kiss on my forehead. "I'll see you soon, Leah," he frowns in concentration

I watch him leave, and my heart aches to call him back to me. Is it something I said? Should I not have asked about Owen? I just need to know he would not be able to hurt me again.

When my parents leave, I sit in the hospital room listening to nurses chattering merrily down the hallway. I hate being hospitalized. Every ache reminds me of what happened. I couldn't defend myself. I didn't think

I had to. I didn't realize that a person could snap the way Owen did. He'd lost his senses. I remember the crazed look in his eyes as he stood above me. The determination he held that mortar with. Long gone was the man I once married and loved for so many years of my life. He was a man driven by hatred, greed, and desperation. I lived with Owen for years and I never once considered that he could turn against me this way. If Leo hadn't arrived when he did, I probably wouldn't be here.

A police woman took my statement earlier and my parents recoiled at my reenactment of what had happened to me. She assured us that there was a good chance that he would be imprisoned for a long time given that I had cameras in my house and a witness. They would have to wait for him to recover to make a proper assessment of the motives behind his actions. I guess all he needed was the right circumstance and the mask he'd worn for so long, finally slipped. I was scared about the future and facing him again when he was on trial.

She emphasized that I could get a restraining order against him even after he has served his sentence. I cried at the thought that he would be able to walk free someday and cause me harm. I let my father hold me and promise me that Owen would not get near enough to harm me. The thought of it sent shivers down my spine.

I need to pull myself together. I wipe away the tears from my cheeks and remind myself that it is over now, that Owen would get the punishment he deserves, but I wonder if that would be enough to keep him from hurting me again.

LEO

"You know you shouldn't be doing that right?" Scott motions to my glass and takes a sip of his beer.

"Fuck off, Scott," I growl, not caring if he gets angry with me.

"Just saying, man." He puts his hands up in surrender. "So you're going to tell me what's the deal, what brought you and whiskey together this early or you're going to be a grumpy asshole?"

I hadn't been to the hospital since I left in the early hours of the morning. I went to the station and went home to crash. I got up around three p.m. and came straight here. I needed a drink and I didn't care what the side effects would be.

"It's Leah." I take another sip. "Last night her soon-to-be ex tried to off her, he beat her up pretty bad and if I hadn't got there when I did, I doubt she'd be recovering in a hospital right now."

"That's messed up, Leo. Where the fuck is this guy?

Someone ought to teach him a lesson,"

"I beat him into a coma of sorts." I smirk, with confidence I don't feel.

"Good on you, man," he slaps me on the shoulder. "I'm sorry, Leo. I'm glad she's alright though,"

"That's just the thing, I'm angry that this had to happen at all. I should have been there to protect her. I should have known something was off." I slam my fist against the hard table. "I sat outside her house for hours while she was inside with that piece of shit."

"Whoa, Leo, you can't blame yourself for something that asshole did. You were there when it counted. You made sure she's still here, some people don't get that chance, man." He looks at me intently.

"But what happens when I'm not there, Scott? Even if he gets the maximum sentence, which could be five years if he's a first-time offender, which I am sure of, then what? I don't even know if I'll be here then..." My voice trails off and I down my drink and motion for another one.

"Then you help her to take care of herself, Leo, self-defense, something."

"I want to be here, man. For the first time in my life, I want to be here." I stand and reach for my wallet to pay for my drinks and Scott stops me.

"I know how you feel, Leo, maybe not entirely but I know, you could say that I've had some experience in that, just know that she needs support, not just from you but from her family and from what you've told me, they're pretty close." He stops and thinks about his next words. "But for now, she has you and that is more than anyone really needs." He smiles.

"Thank you, man." I shake my friend's hand.

I know what I need to do and where I should be right now.

When I get to the hospital, she is asleep. I watch her for a while and gently stroke her hair. She looks so peaceful when she is sleeping. I feel a deep desire need to protect her and I may know how. I just hope she will agree without a fight, because I am willing to put one up. She stirs and slowly opens her beautiful eyes and the smile she offers me melts my heart. I want to keep that smile on her face. The thoughts of that monster try to resurface but I push them away. This is not about him. It is about Leah and me.

"I missed you." she yawns, reaching out to touch my arm.

"I missed you too." I stroke her cheek gently, sure not to touch the bruises, which are darker now than they were last night.

I want to make all the pain go away. I had to try, somehow, even for a little while.

"How are you?" I whisper.

"Better now," she tells me. "Because you're here."

I take her hand in mine and gently kiss her fingers one by one.

"I'm sorry I didn't come sooner, when did the doctor say you can go home?" I ask.

"Tomorrow morning," she responds. The anxiety is evident from the quiver in her voice.

"Good, because I've been feeling lonely." I grin at her, holding her gaze.

She looks at me confused and it is the most adorable thing.

"You never have to go back to that house, Leah, that's not your home anymore. My home is yours and when you're ready, you'll marry me, but until then all you need to do is rest and get better." I kiss her cheek gently.

"Is that supposed to be a proposal, Leo?" She smiles at me tiredly. I look down at her, wanting to protect her forever with everything I am.

"That is a promise, Leah." I take her small hand in mine. I imagine slipping a ring onto her finger soon. "A promise of infinity, and if you consider marriage to be that, you'll have that."

I kiss her eyelids as they close in relief, knowing that I mean every word. I will make sure that she is okay as long as I am here, and I would fight to be here for as long as I possibly could, and when I wasn't, I'd make sure someone else watched out for her, and I know just who I could count on.

LEAH

This is one of the happiest days of my life. I feel incredible. The early morning sunlight shines through the windows of my perfectly lit hotel room. I step outside and feel the faint warmth of it kissing my cheeks. It is still early so no one else is awake. Except my mother, she would be up and fussing already. I smile and take in the stunning view of the ocean before me and let the gentle breeze caress my body. It is truly a breathtaking day, in many ways. I did not want to rush any part of it. I want to savor each moment and in doing so. I want to savor each breath. A year ago, I didn't realize that all this was even a possibility. I didn't realize that second chances existed, but I'd gotten that. Leo gave that to me. Today was the day I would be marrying the love of my life and man of my dreams. To say that I am happy, feels inadequate. There are not enough words which can truly express the way he makes me feel. He was a light in my darkest hour.

I hear the sound of bustling in my room and think that I never should have given Bea the spare key. I roll my eyes and sigh.

"Jog time, lady," she sings it like it is some kind of gift instead of pure torture. "Don't look at me like that, it's just around the block, get that adrenalin level up, get you all pumped up and ready for action." She wiggles her eyebrows.

Bea, my beautiful best friend, believes that there is no better start to the most important day of your life than with an early morning jog. It apparently releases all the happy endorphins that I would need for the big day. Having Bea here is just what I need and I pull her into a hug just to let her know it. Words are not necessary between us. They never were. When my life came crashing down around me, she held out her hand, steadied me with her smile and excessive glasses of wine and slices of pizza.

I pull on a pair of running shorts, a sweatshirt, put on my brightest neon green running shoes, grab some water, and my iPod and we are out of the door in fifteen minutes.

Running down the beach strip with Bea by my side is something spectacular, this early in the morning. The sun is just past the glistening blue water and the yellow and orange of the sky gives the morning a glorious glow. It is a remarkable sight. I keep pushing my body, listening to *Drake* on my iPod and enjoying the view while the sea breeze filled my lungs. I love the sea so much and being here is the one thing that makes me feel grounded. We did a lap as agreed and slow down to a jog until we reach the posh Beach Hotel. I hadn't expected such a magnificent place.

When Leo suggested it to me for our wedding venue, I gawked at the price and told him that I would prove it is overpriced and overrated. It took a whole lot of convincing to get this girl to agree to it. Nevertheless, standing at the entrance now, I am so glad we chose this. It is everything that beauty, elegance and simplicity should be and so much more. The structure stands tall and the lawn practically kisses the shore, I look over to the beach cottages littering the lawn and the one, which is to be ours that night, and I blush. It is all so spectacular.

"Snap out of it, Princess, we've got to get you fed and prepped, honey." Bea hugs me.

I do not care that we are sweaty. I reach out and hug my best friend because I am so grateful for this life.

I check my phone when I get back to the room and I smile.

06:00 Leo: Hey Princess, so, we are about to do this?

06:05 Leo: I have waited for you all my life. I will love you from this moment on, until my last breath, I promise.

06:10 Leo: Still thinking about you, Beautiful.

06:11 Leo: ...and the things I'm going to do to you tonight ;)

I laugh aloud and quickly text back I love you. It is all I need to say. I love him, I truly do, and today we start a completely new journey together. I hop into the shower and by the time I am dressed in shorts and a t-shirt, Bea has prepared my breakfast. Eggs, Bacon, and mozzarella cheese on a slice of whole-wheat toast and a glass of orange juice. She insisted on cooking it herself and not allowing the hotel to cater breakfast for me, in case I get sick on my wedding day. I did not think I was hungry until that first bite. I literally moan with every bite. She laughs and runs off to check on my itinerary. It includes an aromatherapy massage, petal bath, followed by make-up and hair stylists and then photos of the bride and goodness knows what else Leo and Bea have planned. I must be the only bride in the world who hasn't been involved in every detail of her wedding plans.

My mom walks in, takes one look at me and starts to cry immediately. I have to resist the urge to be immature and roll my eyes at her. Mothers can be so dramatic about things like this. There is literally nothing going on yet, just me relaxing on the couch watching reality TV, while waiting for the masseuse. I wrinkle my nose at her then get up to hug and calm her down. It is not the first time I am walking down the aisle. Still, the last time was nothing like this at all. Owen and I were young and settled on a small wedding at the local church and a reception at a nice restaurant. This is the fairytale and I know it. It is not just the glamour. It is the feeling that this is it, my forever.

It's strange how things turn out completely differently than you once planned. When I was a young girl in Greyton, I swore that I would marry Leo the first time he greeted me. It was decided but when I had him, life happened with all its miscommunications and misunderstandings and before I knew it, I found myself married to someone else. Someone I barely knew. The years and experiences taught me that you do not quite know someone until they chose to reveal themselves to you. I wonder whether Owen had been wearing that mask our whole lives and whether just for a second he 'd let his slip. Today is not a day for rehashing all that hurt and pain, today is a day for celebrating new beginnings.

LEO

I miss her. I miss her with every fiber of my being but I can't see her, well not yet anyway. I want to see her. I need to see her. I need to wrap my arms around her and take in her honey and vanilla scent. I need her curls to tickle my nose when I nuzzle her neck. It's our wedding day and I insisted on a traditional approach including staying in different hotels in case I could not resist seeing her. I got up this morning with a headache from hell, but the first thing I thought about was Leah, and that was enough to make me feel better. I sent her a few messages and decide that I need to take a walk, get some fresh air. I see a dozen miss calls from the wedding party but there was one in particular that I was glad I missed. Dr. Evans meant well but he wanted to tell me the same things he always does, cautioning me to do right by Leah. I am doing right by her. I didn't want to talk to him because I didn't want to ruin this day. This is the day I'd been waiting for my whole life.

He did not know that I could not lose her. He did not know that I was so much better now since we got together. He did not see the progress I have made in these last few months. Maybe I am wrong, maybe I should tell her, maybe I should give her the choice, but I need her, I need her to survive. I don't want this death sentence, especially now when all my dreams are coming true, but I have to have faith in hope, there has to be hope, some kind of light at the end of this tunnel. I am a fighter. I am Leo Williams and I never quit. I never give up. Nothing I have ever achieved in life means anything without Leah Jones. She is everything there is, my soul knew that the search was finally over.

I walk around the grounds and I hate that my headache is not lifting. I take some stronger painkillers. It's Kev's fault, dragging me out last night for my last shindig. I may not have had anything to drink but I didn't get much sleep either.

I make my way to the luxurious café downstairs and take a window seat. My best man joins me a few minutes later looking as right as rain. His wife Tania joins us a few minutes later and I understand why. Sex truly is the best hangover cure.

"So we're doing this?" He slaps my shoulder playfully.

"We definitely are bro."

I look at my friend and I am so glad that he is here and that he is so happy for us. Leah and I were not sure how he would take the news of us getting back together but he took it well after a night out, getting drunk and nearly coming to fists with a few people. He is so much more than a best friend. Kevin Jones is my other brother and I love him like that. He was there for me in the early days and we stuck together since, despite the occasional distance. Tania kisses us both goodbye on the cheek, saying she needs to get to Leah. I felt a pang of jealousy. I want to see her wild hair and crooked smile, I want to kiss her lips and tell her that we had our whole life together. My phone beeps and I look at the number, Dr. Evans yet again. I cancel the call and tell Kevin to hurry up because our masseuses await us for a quick relaxation session.

I think about Scott. I asked him to be my third best man.

"Nah, man, weddings gave an ill vibe. Anyway I'm scared Leah may leave you at the aisle when she sees me."

I laughed him off. I understand that there were some things Scott could not and would not talk to anyone about. As if the timing was off anyway, his sister asked him to come stay with her for a few months in London before his new nephew or niece arrived. He could not turn her down. I got that, some of us were fortunate to have amazing siblings. Mine was my second best man who had arrived early yesterday, drank too much last night, and was probably going to be late. I grin at the thought of my little brother, who is not so little anymore.

We enter my suite and our tuxedos have arrived. We each grab a still water and make our way to the make-shift day spa. I think about Leah, that she is probably doing the same thing now. I see her text and smile. Anytime I think of her, I smile. I do not know how I got this lucky but I keep counting my lucky stars anyway. She turned this cold man into something I barely recognize in the mirror lately. I did not know I had a smile for a number of years, but she changed that. I would do anything for that woman. She deserved a Prince Charming and she would get that, I would give her the world. She had my heart from that very first kiss and she had it ever since. My phone buzzes on the table next to me, causing me to tense up.

"You okay, man?" I hadn't realized Kevin was watching me.

"I'm good, just work stuff." I shrug it off and try to relax as the masseuse kneads my tense muscles. My headache is growing worse by the second and I make a mental note to take more painkillers.

After our massages, Kevin grabs his suit, and I walk him out. He stops at the door and puts a hand on my shoulder.

"I love you, man, and I am glad you're the one that's marrying my sister today," he holds my gaze. "You always tell me that you were lost before her, but I want you to know that she was searching for you too. I have not seen her this happy in a long time, so thank you, Leo."

I hug him because he doesn't know how much it means to hear him say that. I pat his back as he leaves. My phone buzzes yet again and I know I cannot ignore him much longer.

LEAH

I have heard people say that girls dream about their wedding dresses since they are little. That they visualize it and when the time is right, they recreate it. I have never been one of those girls, but in that moment when I unzip mine, I understand why girls dream of this moment. I'd seen it at the fittings, but seeing it like this, on my wedding day, in this room, with my family and friends around me, is something else.

The perfect white lace and flowing accents captivate me yet again. The bodice with its incredible miniature pearls and crystals is magnificent and made to fit just perfectly. I run my fingers over the glorious fabric and my eyes glaze over with tears. I would truly be a Princess in that.

I could see my mother watching me, her cheeks wet with newly fallen tears, and I know that this is that moment for me. I walk over to her open arms and I let the pent-up tears fall. I am truly happy. I hear Bea coming up the stairs announcing the arrival of Bronwyn, my makeup artist, and Juan, my hair stylist. I pry myself from my mother's arms and touch her cheek to let her know that having her here is just what I need. My makeup artist and stylists are both godsends and work like professionals while continuously calling me their ultimate chef-d'oeuvre. Our photographer, Jay Jay, is one of the best photographers in the country, renowned for turning the most unlikely moments into masterpieces. He is a burly young man with an easy way and a kind smile, his ear-length hair brushed back and hidden under a cap. I am beyond thrilled that we landed him, although I wasn't surprised, there is nothing Leo wouldn't do to make this day perfect. He had been snapping shots since my morning run according to Bea. I hoped those sweaty and disgusting pictures would not find their way into my wedding album.

11:30 Leo: See you soon Princess. For Infinity.

11:31 Me: For Infinity.

"Put that away," scolds Juan, and I place my phone on the dresser. I laugh and close my eyes to let them finish off. In just a few hours, I would see Leo, and we would begin our forever.

"You can't look in the mirror yet," my stylists tell me once they've completed their masterpiece. Jay Jay starts snapping shots of me in my gown. Juan and Bronwyn start working on my wedding party. I am pleased for the peace and quiet. I need to collect my thoughts.

Leo, my first love and my first heartbreak. I think about that and I smile. When I first met him, I didn't know that he would come to mean so much to me. When he reentered my life, I was going through the worst time in my life. He was the boy who pretended that I did not exist, the boy who made me blush on countless occasions when he caught me staring at him. He was the one I wrote about in my diary and the one I hated for a very long time. He was the man who stole my heart and almost crushed it and then he became my savior, he became the reason I could breathe again. In a time when I felt like my world was crashing down all around me, he held out his hand to steady me, and every day I am glad I took it. I finally realize that love simply is, it cannot mold to one definition. It is everything there is.

LEO

I feel dizzy, very dizzy, and nauseous. The nausea hits me hard, and I cannot breathe. I grab hold of the bathroom sink and suddenly I am emptying out the contents of my stomach. I hold on tight because I cannot breathe. I cannot see. I feel so cold, this cannot be happening, not now, not today, please, somebody help me. Please, it gets darker, the room is closing in on me and for once in my life, I am scared.

An hour earlier...

"Dr. Evans, it's Leo," I am frustrated that I am having this conversation at all.

"Leo, thank you for calling back, where were you, I've been trying to get hold of you for days?"

"It's not a good time, as you can imagine, it's my wedding day."

"Leo, you really should rethink this," he says worriedly.

"What I think is that you should quit playing God and just be my doctor." I put my hand to my temple to soothe the growing headache.

"Your latest tests results are in, Leo," he tries to placate me.

"And what does it say?" I ask, annoyed.

"It's worse than we thought, Leo, the cancer, it's spreading more rapidly," he says frantically.

"Thank you. Dr. Evans," I hold the phone away.

"Leo, we don't…" I hear him say before I cut the call.

I don't want to hear it. I don't want to hear that I don't have time, because I do, we do. We have forever.

At eleven-thirty, I text Leah. Her reply has me smiling. My head hurts and I walk into the kitchen and grab a glass of water, after rummaging through my medicine bag, I find some of the good stuff and gulp it down with water. I make my way to the balcony and just breathe in the fresh air.

The day Kevin told me he was getting married was the day I received my test results, brain cancer, harsh I know. At first it was just the sleepiness, which I thought might be the fact that I was overworking but then there were the headaches, extreme confusion and finally, the seizures. Still it was nothing to be concerned about, thinking back I realize that maybe if I had caught it on the onset, I could have done something about it. A few months ago, tests revealed that it was a malignant tumor growing and spreading aggressively, overpowering my once healthy cells by taking their space, blood, and nutrients. I found out this morning that it had spread to other parts of the body, that I had no time. I was in denial for a long time but the symptoms got worse and I felt like shit a lot of the time. I feel better with Leah, no, I feel healed. She makes my life better. She makes everything okay.

I promised her forever. I promised her that I would give her infinity. I would give her everything she had not had before. How could a love like ours end, and like this? This cannot be it for us. All that time we wasted, all that time she was with someone else who did not know how to treat her the way I do, or love her the way I do. No, this could not be it for us. But as I try to steady myself in the bathroom, sliding down to the tile floor for support, I wonder if it might be.

LEAH

To describe it eloquently, it is magical. Looking at myself in the full-length mirror, I cannot believe the vision before me. How can any woman deny her beauty, grace and elegance on a day like this? I do a little swirl and the dress dances with me. It whispers Leah in every seam. It fit me beautifully from my bosom down to where it touches my feet. The dress hugs me gently and sparkles with every move. It is beyond a doubt exquisite. I imagine the brides of old, those closer to home, those to come in the future, in this moment we are all connected. It is breathtaking. My long curly hair is swept to the side in an elegant style. A crystal tiara graces my head, a gift from Bea. The hairstyle is perfect and shows off my neckline. My mother's crystal earrings and necklace serve as something borrowed, the pieces were delicate, not too much, but just enough. The stunning blue sapphire tennis bracelet from Kevin, something blue, and my grandmother's ring, something old. "Before you forget," my dad's voice drifts in. He hands me an old British sixpence. I run into his arms and almost smudge my makeup.

"Thank you, Dad," I whisper.

"Anytime, Lee bear." He kisses my temple.

My dad was hard on himself after the news of Owen and my problems surfaced. He was distraught that I went through everything I did alone. That caused a rift between us and we barely spoke since then. Now, seeing him here and being a part of my day is so much more than I could have hoped. He looks dashing in his simple tuxedo. I hug him once more and take in the room. My mother is wearing a beautiful baby blue dress suit and looks as graceful as ever. Her hair swept up in a fancy bun. Tania and Bea looked gorgeous in their off-shoulder sapphire blue dresses. They looked sexy and perfect. They let their hair fall, Bea's black a contrast against Tania's red. Is this really happening?

"Tell me this is real guys?" I sigh in relief.

"It is!" they shout in unison.

I walk over to each of them for a brief hug, holding back the tears of joy threatening to fall over any minute.

This is it.

LEO

LEO! LEO!

I hear the muffled voices. It sounds so far away. I'm cold, really cold. It's like I can feel every part of me turn to ice. I remember the story of the young boy who fell into a lake while ice fishing with his parents on holiday. He survived but he described the experience of it to be like ice needles pushing their way into your skin all at once. You can feel it all and you beg for the pain to stop. This is not just pain. I'd felt pain before. This is something far worse.

LEO! I GOT YOU BRO!

Those voices again. I must be dead, I have to be, and it's so cold here. I think I'm being lifted, there is noise everywhere. Noise I can't make out, but it must be noise because it hurts my ears and it hurts my head. I want it all to stop. I just want it all to stop, the cold, the pain, the noise, the fear. I can smell blood, so much blood. I'm choking. I can't breathe. If I'm dead, why does it hurt this bad. I'm tired, I need to sleep. I need to close my eyes and go to sleep. I can't breathe, but maybe if I sleep a little, it'll all be okay.

Wait, I need to rehearse my wedding vows. *Leah!* I shout her name but I don't think anyone hears me. I am tired. I close my eyes and welcome the darkness.

LEAH

I'm sitting in the holding room which is beautiful and overlooks the ocean. In less than half an hour, I will be walking down the aisle and marrying my Leo. I sit on a high stool and my dress flows around me. My bridesmaids have been gone for too long and I am hoping that Bea hasn't convinced Tania to get drunk to get off the nerves. My mom and dad sit quietly on the sofa, and they look so content. The urge to check my phone for the hundredth time is strong, but that would mean getting up in my Jimmy Choo wedding shoes. A few minutes later, Bea bursts in and the flush on her face and tear filled eyes have me flying up.

"What's wrong?" She bursts into tears. She never cries. Tania follows close behind and places her hand steadily on my arms.

"It's Leo, Leah, he's not well and Kevin and Liam are taking him to the hospital right now."

Bea pulls it together and takes me in her arms.

I don't cry.

I won't cry.

Leo will be fine. He has to be. I let Bea hold me. I straighten up.

"Take me to the hospital." I look at them all coldly. They are faces in a crowd now, and I am searching for the one person I don't see.

It can't be now. Not now.

I exit the room and everyone follows close behind me. We get into the limousine parked out front and my dad asks the driver to take us all to City Hospital.

"What happened?" I ask looking out of the window, not wanting to make eye contact with anyone.

"He just collapsed," Bea said softly. "Liam and Kev found him passed out."

"It must be the exhaustion, he's been having those headaches again," I tell them.

I see their glances of concern but I do not care. They may have seen him worse for wear a few minutes ago, but I know him and I know he will be alright. He has to be.

"He'll be good to go, just wait and see," I say tightly. "We can trust Leo to make a scene on our wedding day of all days."

I straighten the creases on my dress, reach for one

of two glasses, and pop the champagne that had been chilling for our departure to the beach cottage for the night. We will do all this tomorrow. We can get another bottle of champagne. It will all be okay.

We pull up at the hospital entrance and I do not wait for my door to be opened instead I throw it open and barge in through the revolving door, ignoring the stares.

"Yes, I'm a fucking bride in a wedding dress with a bottle of French Champagne," I yell, flipping everyone off.

I walk toward the front desk and ask for Leo Williams.

"Who are you to the patient, Miss?"

"As if the fact that I am standing in the hospital reception area in a wedding dress isn't the first clue bitch," I growl at the stupid woman.

"She's his fiancée," my dad chimes in apologetically.

She nods, shaken, and proceeds to check her computer, seconds pass, no minutes, how long have I been standing here? An eternity.

I want to do something, I want to reach over the counter and turn the computer toward me.

"He's in ICU, 5th floor." Her hands shake uncontrollably.

I turn on my heels and within a few minutes I'm at

the elevator, I hit the 5th floor button and wait.

My family comes up behind me but no one dares touch me, not now. I make a break for the stairs and I take them two at a time, I hear a rip but I don't care, I need to get to Leo.

LEO

I am dead.

Except I can hear Kevin and Liam, it isn't clear what they're saying, but I am sure it's them. I open my eyes slowly and I look at them. I want to open my mouth to speak but I can't, so I blink. I can't feel my body. It must be the pain medication because I know that the pain is lurking under there. I look around me, my eyes trying to adjust to the light.

"I answered your phone, it was Dr. Evans," Liam starts. I make that out but it's muffled, unclear, but there's tears streaming down his cheeks and he's talking fast now. Kevin holds his shoulders steadily and I know they know.

The smell of antiseptic is strong and machines are beeping all around me. I feel like I'm in a fog but I know I'm not dead, not yet anyway, I'm in the hospital and my brother and best friend know I'm dying.

They know. "He's on his way." I blink because I can't respond. I don't have the energy to. Who are they talking about?

Leah, Leah, *I shout in my head.* And right on cue, she bursts into the room, her wedding dress all around her, her hair falling around her face. She looks like an angel. *No, I'm not supposed to see you yet, not like this.* She drops into a seat at my bedside and the tears silently fall from her eyes, she is hurting, I can see that, I want to wake up, I want to hold her, and I want to tell her that everything is going to be okay but I cannot do that now. I can't.

Oh, Princess. I'm so sorry, so fucking sorry.

LEAH

Up until the point I walk into the room and see Leo lying on that bed hooked up to all sorts of machines, I didn't want to admit that something is wrong. This feels like a bad joke and I am ready to expose it. However, I didn't expect that the color would be drained from him or the bruises that materialized suddenly. I didn't expect to see his eyes hollow and his body weak. I didn't expect any of it so when I see him, the life drains from me and I suddenly lack the energy to stand. Before I know it, the tears were falling from my eyes and I am unable to breathe. I didn't want to breathe again, not without him.

I sit on the stool next to his bed and take his hand in mine.

"What happened to him Kevin? Liam?" I whisper, knowing most of the answer already, placing my other hand over my brothers as it rests on my shoulder. I look up at him and there is such sadness in his eyes.

"We went to get him and he'd collapsed on the floor, it couldn't have been long though. He was in and out of it but I could tell it was serious. He kept saying his head hurt. But there's more, Leah but I think it's best that his doctor talks to you about it," Liam says.

"No, you tell me, tell me whatever you know, Liam, please," I beg him. I could see the battle raging inside of him. He takes my hand and leads me outside.

Everyone is standing out there, Bea, Tania, my parents and a few others. I smile weakly and Liam and I walk to a quiet corner.

"Leah, I answered Leo's phone and spoke to Dr. Evans, he is his Oncologist."

I feel my chest constricting and I lean against the wall.

"He has Cancer, Leah. Brain Cancer."

"It's a mistake," I grit my teeth. "It has to be."

"His doctor has been trying to convince him to tell you, but he didn't want to, he didn't want to lose you, he didn't want you to marry him because you pity him." He looks at the ground when he says this.

"He told him that?" I ask in disbelief.

"Dr. Evans and Leo are good friends, not just patient and doctor, and they talked," he says sadly.

I start pacing. What the fuck do I do?

"He'll need better treatment then, he'll need to take care of himself better," I say.

"Leah," he grabs hold of me. "He's dying. It's malignant and it's spreading rapidly."

How do you describe that feeling? The one of hope leaving you, it happens when you realize that the one person you cannot live without and love more than life is dying, that they would leave you and there is nothing you can do to stop it. It feels like free falling backward, blindfolded with no safety harness. You know you are going to hit the ground and you know it's going to hurt, you just don't know when and mostly, you don't know if you will survive it. Maybe it will crush your bones, maybe it will make you bleed, but one thing is for sure, you will never be whole again.

I know Leo is sick, of course I know. I had known for a long time. He tried to hide it from me but I knew, but hearing people say it out loud felt different somehow. I am in the medical field. I am not a doctor but I knew. I saw the pills, I heard his hushed conversations. I knew why he went away from time to time. I knew all that and I respected that he was not ready to tell me yet. I never pitied him. I wanted to be with him every day of our lives, no matter how little we had left. That is what love was, in sickness, in health, until death do us part. Wasn't that the deal?

I walk back into Leo's room and leave Kevin and Liam to explain the things I barely know how to comprehend to my family. I feel like I am walking on air, that my feet are not touching the ground. I sit at his bedside quietly, watching him, his eyes closed, his breathing shallow, and I assume he is asleep.

"Don't leave me, Leo, please," I plead as the tears fall down my cheeks and pool under my chin. I don't attempt to wipe them away. I need them as a reminder that my world is falling apart. I believe that he is sick but at the same time, I didn't. Leo is healthy and strong and we have our whole lives ahead of us. He fought this far and he would fight some more.

Infinity, we promised each other that.

"Leah," his voice breaks through the silence.

"Hey, baby," I whisper, placing my hand against his face.

"I'm sorry." He coughs. "I…I thought I had more time, we had more…" he wheezes.

"Shh, baby, you've got to rest, I'm here, not going anywhere," I sob.

"You're beautiful, so beautiful," tears glaze his beautiful eyes. I want the tears to stop. I want the sadness in his gaze to disappear.

"In this old thing?" my voice breaks as I try to tease him.

"Every day, Leah, always," he promises.

LEAH

Leo never left that hospital, but the two months we had together after that fateful wedding day were everything. I would camp out at the hospital daily and I even had a recliner in his room. It became my home. Anywhere Leo was, was home. It did not matter that medical staff surrounded us or that we smelt like antiseptic. All that mattered was that we were together.

We played cards and I read to him from *Sense and Sensibility* and *Pride and Prejudice* to fill our days. He hated Mr. Darcy. I never did understand why, but there would always be things about Leo I would never understand. It is what made Leo, Leo.

Liam and Leo spent a lot of time together. They would watch old karate movies and laugh until the nurses scolded them for not keeping the noise at a respectable level. They flirted with the nurses shamelessly. It was wonderful to watch them. Liam reminded me so much of Leo, except his eyes. We spent a lot of time with Dale and she would tell me all the stories about Leo's time with her. He would frown and shake his head.

A month after he was hospitalized, I insist that we go through with the wedding, it is what I want. I didn't want my dress go to waste, I told Leo one night.

And so, I married my soulmate one beautiful summer day in the hospital chapel in the presence of our families and close friends. The room was small but cozy. The wood floors were scattered in rose petals and every pew had pink and white orchids hanging from them. Even more orchids hung like curtains from the ceiling with angel lights tangled in them.

It was the best day of my life, and it was better than I ever imagined. My dad walked me down the aisle in my incredible beautiful dress and when I looked at Leo, I knew that he would be my forever love always, my infinity. Nothing would change my love for him.

Even though he was weak, he refused to have a wheelchair at our ceremony. He stood beside me, holding my hand and never took his eyes off mine and as I said my vows, I meant every word…

My love,
There are no words to describe what being here with you today feels like
If there were any, they would be inadequate

Because no words can express the feeling of content and euphoria, I feel
You were the first man I loved and you will be my last
You were my savior and you were my shield
When I thought reigniting love was impossible
You proved me wrong
So today, I pledge my love for you
In the presence of our families and friends
to have and to hold you,
from this day forward,
for better and for worse
for richer and for poorer,
in sickness and health,
for not even death could do us part.

I choked up on the last line and there were no dry eyes in the room. I held his hand. He took it to his lips and the electricity in that simple touch was as intense as it has ever been.

My dear, Leah,
Before you, I had not truly lived
But now that I do not have as much time as I would like to
I know that there was no life before you and there will never be a life after
This here is where my heart lies,
This here is where my soul will remain

With you, in your eyes and in your heart
I will never truly leave you
Because forever cannot die
My love for you is forever
Today I pledge my love for you
In the presence of our families and friends
to have and to hold you,
From this day forward,
For better and for worse
For richer and for poorer,
In sickness and health,
For not even death could do us part.

We had a small reception, which Leo and I left about an hour into. Walking into our hospital room, I burst into tears. It was converted into a mini hotel suite complete with a king size bed, lavish mini bar and coffee machine. It was beautiful.

We made love that night, slow and tender, taking time to remember, taking time to forget, he was stronger than he had been in weeks and I loved the taste and feel of him around me, inside me, and beneath me. Later that night, I laid my head on his chest and I willed for more of him, more time, more. Just a little bit more. My tears soaked his t-shirt and he ran his hands through my hair.

"In another lifetime, Princess."

I loved being married to Leo. We picked fights just for the fun of it. I cooked him meals that the doctors approve off and I read to him every chance I got. He grew weaker and weaker and I knew that I would have to say goodbye soon, but I didn't prepare for it when the time came.

My Leo died in his sleep one night while I lay beside him. I woke up the next morning and he was gone. I cried silently and wished to follow. I held onto him until I was pried away by the nurses.

2017
Present Day

"My head said you'd ruin me
and my heart welcomed the demise."
-Jo-Anne Joseph

LEAH

This is why I find myself here today, in this hotel room.

"Infinity, Leo, that's what you promised me!" I shout angrily, throwing a glass at the wall.

I fall to the floor, the grief and sadness hits me in waves. I want to see him just one more time.

I knew he was dying but that did not make it any easier when the time came. I woke up with his arms wrapped tightly around me, his cold lips against my forehead. I thought I would scream when he left me. There was no sound. I held on tighter, I let the loss of him burn into my skin and my soul. The tears streamed down my cheeks and I let them, they fell on his gray sweater and I snuggled closer. I can't remember now how long I was lying like that but a strange coldness reached my bones. I lay there holding onto the love of my life and I willed him to wake up, to breathe for me.

The nurses came in and pried me away. I didn't stop crying, there was no sound escaping my lips, just the tears. I sat rocking on the recliner when my brother arrived and he held me close and I looked him in the eye and never uttered a word. My parents arrived, Liam arrived, and everyone held me close. They kissed my Leo goodbye. I knew I never would. Goodbye was not something Leo and I did. I watched the undertakers come in for My Leo, I wouldn't say a word. "Are you his wife?" I didn't say anything, just rocked myself. My brother answered, Liam answered. I had nothing more to say.

I went home, to our home, without him, Bea by my side, I held his belongings in my hands. Bea walked me upstairs and told me to take a shower and that she would be up in a few minutes. I got into his side of the bed and I lay there. I wouldn't shower. I wouldn't wash him off me. I needed to feel him near me. I cried into his pillow, his scent was everywhere, earth and Leo, earth and Leo. There was no earth without Leo, there was no me without Leo. Bea came in and she lay behind me, she wrapped her small arms around my waist and I felt her small shakes as she cried and cried for her best friend's loss.

I fell asleep and when I woke up everything was dark. I hadn't spoken in hours, my insides clenched with what I assumed was hunger. I closed my eyes again. Someone woke me and gave me a tablet.

"To calm you." I didn't know who it was but I took the tablet anyway.

I was calm but maybe I would fade into nothingness if I was so lucky. There was food on a serving tray, the smell made me queasy. I let the darkness swallow me.

I don't know what to do next, where to go. I don't know if I can live again without him. There is only so much heartache one person can take. For me, I don't see how I can survive this. How do I begin to live as my friends and family tell me to, when I can barely stand? How do I live without a piece of myself, how do I even begin to walk again when breathing is so difficult?

Leo took everything from me. He took my will to live and my will to survive.

I go to open another bottle but the nausea is strong and I run to the bathroom to hurl out the contents of my stomach. I do not feel so good.

I grab my phone and text the only person I can stand to see right now.

Bea, I need you.

I sit down on the bathroom floor and I feel faint, dizzy. I know I am going to collapse and so I lie down on the cold floor and wait for the darkness to take me.

It was a dull day, an ugly day, it rained and rained. I couldn't walk into the church myself so my brother and Liam were my vices. I didn't need a vice, I needed my anchor. I hadn't eaten in days, I didn't know how this funeral came to be, someone planned it, someone ordered white roses and they were everywhere, the smell was sickening. Leo hated church, I laughed to myself won-

dering what he would say about all this. **It's fucking madness, Leah.** *I shook my head at the sound of his voice.* **You're not here, you can't do anything about it, hotshot.**

There is a casket up front and they walk me to the front row and I sit down, I can see that the casket is open and his nose peeks out. **I look like shit,** *he complains.* **So do I, so I guess it's okay.** *Faceless people come to hold my hand and offer their condolences, I nod, I don't speak, and I don't smile. I don't have the energy for that. I'd had one shower in days and that nearly killed me.*

There is a minister up front, a handsome man and I wonder what made him want to become a Minister anyway. I wonder if he has a smooth chest or one with freckles on it, like Leo. **That's a messed up thought babe, he's a collared man.** *He talks about things I can't really comprehend. Calls Leo his brother, talks about eternal life and then I can't concentrate. I get up and walk toward the casket and there must be gasps. I feel someone behind me. I get to him and he doesn't look like Leo, he's so pale and gray and is that make-up. I smile at the mannequin of my Leo and close the casket. I don't care if it's time, it's time for me and I leave the church and I start walking. I start walking as far as my feet can carry me and then when I can't walk anymore, I find a bench and let the rain wash away every silent tear.*

I wake up to an incessant beeping sound. There are hushed voices, and the strong antiseptic smells tell me

I'm in hospital. Why couldn't I have gotten lucky and died. Maybe I am finally dying, but if that is the case, it wouldn't explain the fact that I actually feel alright. I open my eyes and I'm groggy. The light hits me and I want someone to turn it off or close the curtains, whatever the source of this torture is.

"Leah, honey, how are you feeling?" The sound of my best friend's voice brings me to reality.

"Bea, where am I?"

"In the hospital, hon, I came over as soon as you called but you'd already passed out on the bathroom floor. I brought you here."

"Thank you, Bea," I try to smile.

I am grateful that she is here. I'd shut myself off from the world for so long, it felt good to see a familiar and caring face.

"Ms. Jones?" a tall burly man with a baseball cap asks. "I'm Dr. Collins, how are you feeling?"

I notice that he looks nothing like a doctor. I want to correct him. I want to tell him I'm Mrs. Williams but I never got a chance to own that name. I didn't deserve it. If I did, he'd be here. Wouldn't he?

"Are you alright Ms. Jones?" He continues as if that is even a question.

"How do you think I feel, like shit, I'm in a hospital for goodness sake?"

"Leah," Bea scolds me.

"So what's wrong with me?"

"Nothing much, you're just suffering from exhaustion, you drank too much, your blood pressure is very high, insulin level very low, and you're pregnant." He flashes me a million-dollar smile, which might melt the heart of anyone but me.

"Did you say I'm pregnant?" I ask, getting up into a sitting position.

"Yes, among other things." He smiles.

Bea looks at me and the excitement on her face is palpable. It must take her a lot not to pull me into a hug. I, on the other hand, just feel cold, so cold and so fucking alone.

"There must be a mistake, Doctor," I explain.

"Nope, you're exactly four months pregnant but you're carrying small, which is probably why you didn't notice anything. The baby is healthy and strong despite the elevated alcohol levels in your blood. But I would advise that you stay away from the alcohol," he cautions. I am four months pregnant, how is that possible? I didn't get past the twelve week mark the last two times.

He looks at my chart and Bea looks at me as if she is about to burst.

"Congratulations to you and the father," Dr. Collins offers kindly.

Bea's face drops.

"The father is dead, Dr. Collins. But thank you anyway. You should do yourself a fucking favor and not make dumb assumptions," I do not care how shitty that sounds. How dare he?

"I'm sorry, Ms. Jones, I wasn't aware."

"Then you should shut your fucking mouth!" I scream. He doesn't flinch. He doesn't do much of anything. He doesn't even look at me with that pitiful gaze people get when they hear about Leo.

I hate this conversation and I hate this doctor. I hate being here in this hospital, I hate being anywhere Leo is not which sucks because that would be just about everywhere.

"I have to go," I try to get out of bed to leave and start to pull the drip off my arms.

Dr. Collins' strong hands close around my shoulders. "Ms. Jones, we need to keep you and the baby here for overnight observations."

"I'm fine, just tired," I tell him brusquely. "I need to leave and I need to be alone."

"Ms. Jones, I am afraid that's against hospital policy, you will have to sign an indemnity if you do leave of your own will, putting yours and the life of your child at risk."

I can sense his patience slowly diminishing.

"Just stay the night, Leah," Bea chimes in. "What harm is it going to do to let them monitor you for the night? Please." Her eyes are imploring me to see reason and I relent, remembering how much stress I probably put her through today.

"Okay." I get under the covers once more. "But I need to be alone."

Bea gets up and kisses my forehead. "I love you, Leah, and I am just one call away." With that, she leaves.

"I'll be back to check on you later. You'll be okay, Ms. Jones," Dr. Collins states. He hesitates at the door but thinks better of whatever he wants to say.

I place my hand over my belly, noticing a tiny bulge, one that no one else would be able to notice. I think about the life growing inside me, the life that Leo and I created four months ago. A baby who will never know his father, a baby whose mother is broken into a million pieces. A shell of the person she used to be.

"How could you leave me, Leo?" I cry into my uncomfortable hospital pillow. "How?" And then I wait for an answer which will never come.

2019

"There is nothing on earth or beyond,
That could sever the bond between us,
You are and forever will be,
My best friend and soul mate,
Forever"
-Jo-Anne Joseph

LEAH

Two years later…

“Ready or not here I come,” I shout loudly.

“Leo, where are you, you little rascal?” I laugh as I search for my son. He gives terrible two a completely new meaning. I wonder where he is right now, actually hiding or crawling under the fence to harass the neighbor’s cat.

“I’m not here, Mommy,” his little voice calls back to me and I know he is behind the greenhouse.

“Peek-a-boo, where are you, I think I may have found you,” I whisper as I pick him up squealing in delight.

It’s his second birthday party. Leo is just like his father in every way. He has the same brown eyes and dark brown hair that falls into his eyes, that infectious smile and a dimple on his right cheek. He speaks incredibly fluently for a two-year-old which surprises most people we meet.

"Everyone will be arriving anytime now, Leo, we've got to go inside and get ready, sweetheart," I pick him up and swing him over my shoulder. He laughs and tries to wriggle free.

"One more hour. Mommy, please," he begs.

"You always say that, Leo." I laugh.

"You two." Bea laughs and shakes her head when I enter the kitchen with my mud covered little boy. She's putting the finishing touches to her homemade pizza and hamburgers. My best friend has been my saving grace over the last three years. She has been the constant in the raging storm that has been my life. She is the one who held my hand when I gave birth to my healthy breathing baby boy and she is the one who cried with me on that first night alone in Leo's house with our son just down the hallway. She is also the one who helped me make this house a home for Leo and me.

I walk into the living room and Leo wriggles from my grasp and runs over to the pictures on the family wall.

"Daddy, it's my birthday," he says to a picture of Leo.

It is a picture of Leo at Kevin's wedding. He is strong, handsome and so full of life in the shot. Our son walks over to a picture of me sitting on Leo's lap on our wedding day, our faces turned to each other, smiling giddily. You would not know that he was unwell, you would not know that he had just a month to live, you cannot tell those things from pictures. They paint scenes of perfection.

However, the sadness reflected in my eyes since then is undeniable, especially in those early pictures with our son. It still breaks my heart, the fact that Leo is absent from our lives, and that he is not here to watch our beautiful son grow up. Leo gave me the greatest gift in the world, he saved me, he destroyed me, but then he unknowingly revived me and it is because of that, that I arose, like a Phoenix from the ashes, stronger and above all alive. I still have my bad days. I still drown my sorrows in a bottle when my son is asleep every now and then. I can't deny that. When you experience a great loss like I did, you can't be expected to bounce back and be the same person. You change as a human being. You see things differently, more clearly even.

This is by no means the story that I envisioned for my life and this wasn't the story I'd asked for, but it is mine all the same, and I take it wholeheartedly.

"Yes, baby boy." I smile at my beautiful little boy. "Daddy knows." I scoop him up again. Leo, I motion to his little chest, Leo, I motion to the picture frame on the wall, "Together forever."

"Infinity," a familiar voice finishes. I look up and

smile at the man leaning against the doorframe. Two years and a pregnancy ago, Scott Collins came into my life so unexpectedly, and over the last year or so he has been a good friend to me. It did not start that way. In fact, I disliked him at first. I sensed that the feeling was mutual. He is not in the scrubs I have been accustomed to seeing him in. He's wearing a pair of blue jeans and a white button down shirt. His dark hair a mess as it always is.

It is such a coincidence that he and Leo used to be friends and that Leo wanted him to be my partner at the Centre. He does incredible work and I respect him for that. Bea is convinced that there is something romantic brewing between us, but Bea would think that. Her head is in the clouds about such things. I am not ready for it. There would never be a replacement for Leo.

From time to time, I wonder what is behind those soft brown eyes and easy smile Scott has. Like he carries the weight of the world on his strong shoulders and he does not have anyone to share it. He is here though and I am grateful for his friendship every day. He is more than just a business partner. He is our friend. Little Leo and Scott adore each other. They keep each other busy and happy.

"Someone needs to clean up, young man." He laughs, taking Leo from me.

“Uncle Scott, I’m clean,” Leo, says smudging mud on Scott’s cheek. Scott starts to tickle Leo until he is almost breathless, begging to go upstairs. I reach out to take Leo.

“I’ve got him,” Scott follows Leo.

The doorbell announces the arrival of family and friends and I rush to let them all in. Kevin and Tania enter, her beautiful face radiant with that early pregnancy glow. I love the idea of Leo having a little cousin soon. I hug them both, and welcome them followed by my parents. I look at them all so fondly and my heart smiles at the love and support they have given little Leo and me over the years. They have a whole bunch of gifts and as much as I want to frown, I smile. I love them all for spoiling my son and being here with us on these incredibly difficult days. Sometimes angels do not have wings you can see, they simply walk with you every day. I know that now, watching them all gather in the back deck.

I walk back to the picture of Leo and I touch his beautiful face, where the dimple is, my favorite place. “I miss you, babe, every day.” And I imagine that he is smiling back at me. ***I miss you too, Princess.*** I don’t hear him anymore, his voice has faded somewhat and the picture in my mind isn’t as vivid. I miss his kisses. I miss his touch. I miss everything about him.

“I wish you could have met him, Leo, been here with

us, but I'm grateful for this life, Leo Williams. Thank you." I smile and make my way into the kitchen. Bea's laughter and Kevin's banter fill the room and give it almost a glow. I will miss him forever but surrounded by these people, I still feel blessed.

LEO

2017

I am watching you now, as you read one of your historical novels to me. I remember the days when that is what I did. Read to you and watch you laugh and cry. I miss the weight of you on my chest. You never climb on me the way you used to but when I hold you close I still feel our souls connecting in a way not many understand. Your hair is wild, just the way I like it. It always looks windswept even if you have not been outside, your eyes are bright and your nose wrinkles every now and then in concentration. You mouth the words you are reading with childlike expression, which often makes me laugh.

You are what I will miss most about this life, your voice is like music to my ears, your touch like a gentle breeze, your mind is always working and wondering, it's what makes me love you most, your thirst for more. You are effortlessly beautiful and sometimes I doubt that you know it. You may not believe it but your love is what saved my soul. I always had one but it was nothing worthy until you. I will miss you more than you will ever miss me and if I am able, I will watch over you always. I will be there in your darkest hours the way you were there for me.

You accepted my illness, my abandonment of you, with such grace, because that is who you are. You are a creature of grace and exquisiteness. I watch you with my brother Liam and I can tell that the two of you will be good friends and look out for each other. He needs someone like you to keep him on track. He knows how much I love you, Leah Williams. He already considers you a sister. I wish so much that we had had more time. More time to discover the things we had missed about each other over the years. The things we took so much for granted. I want to know when you started to cook those mouthwatering meals, when did you stop burning eggs when you boiled them?

You never knew that I liked you the moment I set eyes on you when we were kids. I couldn't admit it then and I never admitted it to you. You were weird crazy even but you were the one person who made me feel important even if it was through your stalking me.

You have always wondered why I hate Mr. Darcy, well, I can finally admit that the smug bastard reminds me a lot of myself, except he gets to stay with his Elizabeth, and he gets to make her happy every day of their lives together. I will not get to do that with you, I have only borrowed time. Still I am grateful for every moment I have spent with you. I am grateful for how you changed me and what you have given me.

I will not be around for much longer, I know that, I can feel it and I am glad that I was able to make some important arrangements for you and your life. You are too independent sometimes and I would never take that away from you but I do need to know that you will be okay in every sense. Liam and Kevin will make sure everything happens the way I want it to, possibly better. I still want to make all your dreams come true, Leah, besides me, of course.

I wish I had introduced you to Scott. He is a good friend of mine with passion to help people the way you do. I know that you will not only work together well but that he will take care of my girl and he will be the best friend you need. That is who Scott is, loyal and caring. He has become special to me and in some ways I want you to be there for him too. He would never agree to any of this if I had thrown it at him, but he will do it because he is a kind bastard.

You are staring at me now with those wondering eyes and I imagine that my silence intrigues you. You have always been that way.

I will love you, Leah Williams, as long as forever.

The End

Acknowledgements

When I was eleven years old, I wrote my own take on the Little Mermaid story for a cute little eight-year-old boy. He loved the book with all his heart and told me that when I grew up I should write books. Here, I am twenty-two years later, writing stories with him by my side. I want to thank you Brian Joseph, my husband and best friend, for believing in me when I could only string together a few sentences per page. I am so grateful for your love and support. Thank you and our son for the time you give me to live my dreams out loud and write stories for the world to read. You are the reason I believe in love stories. After all this time, you are.

To my beautiful son Braydon, one night you told me that it is a good idea that I have to start writing books. I cherish those words and your often subtle excitement for this exciting time in our lives. This book is dedicated to all our dreams. When you read this book, years from now, may you know that there is nothing you cannot do and that it will never be too late. I love you both with all my heart, soul, and words.

To my parents, thank you. I know that you are looking down on me from your place in the spirit world and celebrating with me. I have no doubt that you are insanely proud of me. Mum, thank you for your fighting spirit. It is why I keep fighting.

To my little sister, Janine, I remember how you always said I should write a book and I promised you that I would. You promised you would be the first one to buy it. You're on the clock. You have always cheered me on. I know that, and I will forever love you for it.

To two beautiful souls, my mentors and friends, fellow authors Abby Gale and Dani Rene, thank you for taking time out of your own busy writing schedules to beta read for me, to push me and to motivate me and advise me. There were some things I never asked for, yet you offered it and when I say I am grateful, know I mean it sincerely. I have a high regard for your work and your hearts. Your comments and advice has been invaluable. I will never forget your help.

To all my beta readers and arc readers, thank you so much. Your input and eye for details have been incredible and have truly assisted in enhancing this story.

To my editor and proof reader, thank you for all your work.

To my gorgeous cover girl, my dear friend, Taryn Karrian. Thank you for sharing your beautiful picture with me and the world. Thank you for celebrating with me and all the support you've given me. Your excitement has been contagious. I love you much.

To Mad as a Hatter Author Services (PA's Amanda Hill and Angela Evans) and Indies Ink, thank you for your assistance.

To my ultimate fans, my first unofficial street team members, I cannot thank you enough. You have been cheering for me from day one, Nicole Townsend Brown, Nancy George, Lin Viljoen, Rolene Naidu and my amazing aunt, Mary Gloria Kaessman, thank you for making me feel like a Rock Star.

To my high school English Teacher, Ms. N Habib. Thank you for believing that I could. I never forget how hard you pushed me and how much you believed in me as a student.

And my special thank you is reserved for **you**, my readers. Thank you from the bottom of my heart for taking this chance on me. Thank you for clicking that "buy" button and giving this new author your support. You are all so amazing and I look forward to sharing so much more with you in future. I imagine my book in your hands and I smile, grateful, content, and anxious to know your thoughts.

About the author

Jo-Anne is a self-published contemporary romance author. She loves all things love and romance. She is a sucker for the seemingly impossible, second chances and everything in between. Her lifelong love affair with words started from a young age and blossomed to her debut release of Infinity. Her writing is and will always be her ultimate adventure and escape.

Jo-Anne is also an advocate for the infant and baby loss community. She regularly writes for on-line publication Still Standing Magazine and the website Glow in the Woods. Her articles have been republished in several newsletters. She has contributed to the book, Our Only Time, Edited by Amie Lands, Author.

"There is no greater agony than bearing an untold story inside you."
- Maya Angelou

Stalk Me

Stalk me here to keep up to date
on my new book releases and events:

www.joannejosephauthor.com
Email: info@joannejosephauthor.com
www.instagram.com/joanne.joseph84
www.twitter.com/jjosephauthor
https://www.facebook.com/joannejosephauthor
Pinterest: joannejosephauthor

Destiny

Sometimes I watch her as she goes about her day at the Centre. It's just a job to her, a duty. She comes in late every day and she looks tired and run down. Her curly hair in a low ponytail, her nails are unpainted and uneven, her eyes are surrounded by dark sleep deprived bags. She doesn't have the passion, commitment or heart that's needed for a job like this. I don't know why Leo ever believed in her enough to invest in a venture like this. I guess that is what you do when you love someone, you accept their flaws. And boy, did Leah Jones Williams have many.

The other therapists here were passionate and driven. They were made for this line of work. People love them, the children love them. I can work with them. But Leah isn't like them, no, she is fucking hopeless mess and today, I'm going to tell her that. I don't care if she cries and runs out of here feeling like a failure, because that is what she is. She can't go through life feeling sorry for herself and running this Centre to the ground in the process. That isn't a luxury afforded to many.

She strolls into her office, sinks into her chair and turns on her computer. I can see her clearly from my desk. We have an open door, all glass work space policy. She leans on her desk with both her elbows and puts her chin in her hands and yawns. That woman actually yawned, at work. I don't like her. I'd known her for almost two years now and she is a liability. I don't know how her family can stand to be around her. If she wasn't a majority shareholder, I would fire her ass in a heartbeat. I could walk away but I love what I do too much and I guess I want to carry out my friends last wishes.

Leah is a real Debbie downer. She doesn't light up a room. She drains the life and soul from it. I told Willow about her a few times and all I got was a plea to be gentle with her. I couldn't help but feel like my sister was judging me instead of Leah.

"Leah!" I walk into her office unannounced. I stand in front of her desk with my arm folded across my chest. She looks up at me with those pathetic brown doe eyes and I almost cave and not say what I need to. But this behavior cannot go on. She's obviously hung over again as she is on a daily basis.

"Oh, hi Scott, are you feeling better?" She asks kindly.

"What do you mean, I wasn't sick?" I ask her annoyed.

"No, I mean about earlier this morning." She wrings her hands together nervously. She's always on edge. All the fucking time!

I'm so angry that she brought my near meltdown from this morning up, but I can't let my anger get the better of me. I am a professional. I quit my day job for this.

"We've had some complaints from a few of the parents of the children you treated last week," I start, crossing my arms in front of me. "They feel their kids aren't getting the attention they need and if it doesn't improve they're going to have to see someone else and I can only hope it will still be in this Center."

"I didn't realize…" she starts, mumbling, looking down at her hands in her lap. "I'm sorry Scott."

"I'm not the one you should be apologizing to, Leah, you're wasting people's time, and you're wasting your time." I spit out angrily. "You think you can come in here looking like you just got run over every single day and nobody would notice. You are like the walking dead, Leah, and you are infecting everybody with your negativity."

She flushes, tears forming in her eyes as she gets up and gathers her things to leave. She stops in front of me, straightening up, squaring her shoulders and looking up at me with determination.

"Fuck you, Scott Collins, I don't mean to be this way, I just don't know how else to be without him." She hisses as the tears fall down her cheeks. I tower over her small frame and in that moment I feel like an asshole. Maybe I was too harsh with her.

She storms out of her office before I can say anything. I watch as she walks briskly to the exit without giving me a second glance and for the first time in a long time, I regret my behavior.

www.ingramcontent.com/pod-product-compliance
Lightning Source LLC
Chambersburg PA
CBHW030417180626
46812CB00005B/2052

* 9 7 8 0 6 2 0 7 6 6 9 9 9 *